SECRETS FROM A SHALLOW GRAVE

A JORDAN PARKER COZY MYSTERY
BOOK 2

Liz Turner

Contents

Chapter 1
The Troublesome Lizard

Jordan Parker grinned with delight as she snapped her favorite photograph yet. Ordinary teenage girls might obsess over photographically documenting every angle of their morning cappuccino, but Jordan Parker was certainly no ordinary eighteen-year-old. Jordan's pride was centered, not on how many 'likes' her photograph could earn her on social media, but on the incriminating evidence digitally etched onto her camera's memory card.

Satisfied that she had aptly captured the moment, Jordan pulled her eye away from the lens and relaxed slightly, allowing herself a second to enjoy the scene without the obstruction of her bulky camera.

The red-faced shopkeeper huffed as he heaved another overflowing crate of mangoes into the darkness of the back of his shop. There were still leafy stalks attached to the rich orange fruit, as though each mango had been yanked from their branches. As the man drew another box from the back of his pickup truck, he paused, his dark eyes shooting around furtively as he examined the bush line for movement.

Jordan held her breath, her fingers inching around the collar of a fluffy neck. Shiny brown eyes caught hers, and sharp ears pointed in the man's direction. Jordan shook her head and the foxlike ears drooped again, the brown eyes absorbing her meaning.

Satisfied that there was no one around, the man fired a tar like globule of tobacco from his mouth. It splattered against a rock about a stone's throw from where Jordan hid. This sent a fat, sun-warmed lizard scuttling through the dense green grass. Sharp ears spiked again, followed by the twitch of a wet nose, and Jordan knew it was over.

A snowy white dog pounced out from the cover of the bush and dropped two paws down on the patch of dirt where the lizard had been milliseconds before. The enormous man spun around, sending heavy mangoes toppling out of the box and smacking on the ground. He bellowed at the dog, his dark eyes encircled by a ring of fire, and he advanced with a thick stick in his hand.

"No one hits Ms. Elizabeth Snickles!" Jordan shouted, in time to warn her dog to get out of the way. She positioned herself firmly between Liz and the man.

The man, who was already in the motion of swinging his club when Jordan jumped out of the bushes, stopped the chunk of wood inches from her head. The trouble-causing lizard was safely seated on a branch, his golden eyes watching the entertainment below.

"You!" the man screamed at her. "What are you doing here again?"

Jordan stared at him blankly, her eyes absorbing every twitching muscle on his face as he glared down at her. There was a distinctly purple vein throbbing in the center of his forehead, and his enormous body spasmed with uncontrollable surges of rage. He looked as though he was ready to murder her. Jordan shrugged this terrifying thought from her mind, and she forced the muscles in her limbs to move.

While Jordan usually prided herself on her ability to remain incognito while investigating a case, she had slipped up earlier that day. It had mostly been Liz's fault, the foxlike dog growling at her feet. Jordan had been spying on him, picking up some parcels from an unsavory character earlier that week. Unfortunately, Liz had sniffed out a devilled ham sandwich left unattended on the passenger seat of his truck. Jordan had brushed off the incident as coincidental, but only just. But now, having spotted her and Liz for the second time in the same week, the man's eyes dilated dangerously with suspicion, if not something else.

The man's arm flexed, and he raised his gnarled piece of wood, his dark eyes fixed on his new target, which was considerably less furry. Jordan wasted no time in ducking below his swing, grabbing her dog, and scampering back into the safety of the dense tropical bush that covered most of the island.

At first, all Jordan could hear was her own heartbeat thumping in her ears, but as adrenaline soared through her body, her other senses heightened too. She could hear the furious shopkeeper screeching after her. His voice stopped and then all she could hear was the rhythm of her feet beating against the damp grass and the whip of the tall grass as it stung her arms.

An engine fired up.

An out of breath, Jordan lowered a scrambling Liz to the ground and her other sweaty hand clutched her camera closer. There was no point cracking a case if you did not live long enough to provide the authorities with convincing evidence to back your theories. Jordan knew that if she kept hurtling through the endless bush, she would get lost and run the danger of clambering off the edge of a sudden cliff and join a school of hungry sharks for a swim.

She stopped, gazed at the direction of the lowering sun for a moment, and set off in a different direction. The sounds of vehicles grew louder, and Jordan gasped with relief as she glimpsed the tarmac road leading into town.

"At least we won't be food for…" Jordan paused not only to catch a much-needed breath, but to think of what could hunt her in the wilderness of a small island called Dandelion Drift.

She waved this poorly timed mental distraction away and plunged through the remaining bush line and onto the main road. A car swerved out of the way and missed Jordan by inches. Jordan leapt back onto the grassy sidewalk and sighed in relief at the comfort of being surrounded by other people again. As the driver shoved his torso out the window of his car and shook an angry fist at Jordan, she had never felt happier at being so close to people. What could go wrong in public?

The scream of desperate tires squealing across tarmac provided the answer. The unforgiving shopkeeper drove with half his torso hanging out the window, as he homed in on the meddling girl and her pesky dog. Jordan did a double take and zig zagged to the other side of the road. A newspaper boy swerved his bicycle into the back of a car to avoid hitting her.

Jordan threw a quick glance over her shoulder and noticed that the oncoming traffic had done little to deter the relentless man who was now the shade of plum jelly and mounting the sidewalk on her side of the road.

"Give me that camera you -"

Fortunately, the four-word expletives generously spewed out by the livid man were drowned out by a series of honking from the vehicles having to screech out of the way of the shopkeeper's smoking truck and then dive back into the safety of their own lane.

"You're going to pay for what you did, Mr. Cullen!" Jordan screamed over her shoulder; her voice lost in the surrounding turmoil.

Mr. Cullen's front bumper held back inches from her fleeing feet, and Jordan could hear the manic laughter escaping the cap of his truck. Liz yelped in fright, her big, brown eyes wild with fear. She had faced many dangers in her life as a street dog, but none so terrifying as the ones she had encountered as the adopted sidekick of Jordan Parker, amateur sleuth, and definite trouble magnet on her quest for truth.

Thanks to a brilliantly placed series of streetlights, Mr. Cullen was forced to veer out the way. Jordan tried to take advantage of the gap, but her legs were too tired for her to sprint any longer. Cramps spiked up her calves and her feet felt numb from the repetitive slap against the tarmac. She could hear the familiar growl of the engine as it thundered closer, and she knew Mr. Cullen would not spare her for much longer.

The camera weighed heavy in her hand, and she considered giving up everything she had snooped to find the last couple of weeks. What was one more uncaught criminal in a tumultuous sea of crime? Jordan shook her head. Her throat was dry, and her legs were on fire, but she would not stop just so a thug could get his own way. She thought of the poor farmer, desperate to make ends meet with his tiny mango farm and pleading with her to help catch the thief stripping his trees and running him out of business.

Jordan gritted her teeth and shouted with determination as she kicked forward, desperate to reach another shop, or find a friendly face that could offer her protection. In answer to her pleas, siren lights illuminated the buildings in alternating flashes of red and blue, warning the oncoming cars of a police roadblock. Vehicles around her slowed and obediently joined a single lane as they passed police inspection.

Jordan could just make out the familiar outline of detective Nicolas Turner stepping out into the center of the road, a bullet-proof vest strapped over his shirt and tie, and his weapon aimed at the tire of the speeding truck that smashed through all the police cones and barriers.

Jordan was so relieved, grateful tears mingled with her sweat and wet her fiery cheeks. Her wobbling legs managed the final sprint to the police line, where an officer yanked her behind the shield of a police vehicle door.

"What are you doing here, Jordan?" officer Brown hissed at her.

Jordan was too out of breath to plan intelligible words and black sparks darted on the edge of her vision. Even Liz collapsed onto her side, her ribcage heaving as she tried to suck in air. It forced the truck driver to scream to a halt in front of the armed detective. He foolishly attempted to turn his vehicle round, which only made him appear more suspicious. Turner waved a gun inside the window of the truck and ordered the shopkeeper to step out with his hands behind his head.

"You're interfering in a police operation," Turner informed him. "If you just cooperated -"

"He's a liar and a thief!" Jordan yelled from behind officer Brown.

"What is she doing here?" a tall woman said, stepping out from behind her own vehicle in a pair of lethal red high heels. "She's going to blow everything!"

Nicolas lowered his weapon and dropped his head. "Jordan," he nearly groaned her name, "step forward and explain what's going on."

Jordan shook herself free of officer Brown, delivered a disapproving glare at the blonde woman, and strutted proudly up to detective Turner's side.

"Mr. Cullen," she flung a hand in the direction of the sweating, scarlet-faced shopkeeper grounded with his hands behind his head, "has been stealing mangoes from a poor, local farmer struggling to feed his own family."

The blonde woman laughed with derision in the background. "Now she's done it," she stated gleefully to officer Brown. "Mangoes instead of a heist!"

"Let her explain herself, detective Rain," Nicolas threw over his shoulder, silencing the blonde woman who cast a sneer at Jordan.

"I have proof," Jordan added, after gulping down air and trying to smooth her drenched hair out of her face.

"I bet you do," Nicolas replied with a sympathetic smile. "You always do."

It was the smile adults used on naughty kids when they had clearly done something wrong, but needed a gentle explanation for the reproof to follow.

"The problem is," Nicolas continued, settling clear grey eyes on her, "a few stolen mangoes are not really a criminal offence worth the entire police squad being on high alert."

"You see!" the shopkeeper blasted at Jordan, spittle decorating his plump, chapped lips. "This insane piece of rubbish teenager has been stalking me for the last week, photographing my innocent business ventures!"

"Innocent!" Jordan scoffed, her hands falling onto her hips. "Check the back of his truck, Nick."

The detective raised an eyebrow.

"Detective Turner," she corrected herself immediately, with a respectful bow of her head.

Mr. Cullen was practically frothing with protests. He even tried to scramble to his feet and block the detective's path.

"Not so fast," Turner objected, a slight shake of his wrist reminding the shopkeeper that he held the gun and the badge. A second signal sent officer Brown to the rear of the truck to check for anything suspicious.

"We've got several boxes of mangoes," Brown reported in a dry, unimpressed tone.

"We don't have time for this, Turner!" detective Rain yelled, her gun at the ready too.

"I told you there was nothing serious going on here. Like I tried to explain to this daft girl, I simply have an agreement with the farmer," Cullen informed them with a simpering smile. "If you let me get on my way now, I won't press charges against this immature delinquent."

Nicolas turned his head slightly, a sign that he knew Cullen was lying through his teeth.

"Well, now I know you're lying. Jordan is anything but daft. Jordan," he raised his weapon again at the shopkeeper, "what's really going on?"

Jordan marched to the back of the truck, pushing in front of Brown and overturning a box of mangoes.

"That's my merchandise!" Cullen screamed at her.

Jordan raised her eyebrows and smirked, her hand gesturing casually to the plastic bags containing white powder, lying just visible beneath the scattered heap of mangoes.

"What do we have here?" Brown asked, his pale face blank with confusion.

"Cocaine," Jordan clarified, her arms folding smugly across her chest. "And I have photographs of the miscreants who smuggled it in and sold it to him."

"I've… I've never seen that before in my life," Cullen stammered uncertainly, his porky face paling with panic. "Like I said, I was just delivering these mangoes for the farmer. That powder must be his!"

"Your story changed quickly," Nicolas observed with a scowl. He holstered his gun and reached for a pair of handcuffs.

"I've been following him for far longer than a week. He's been supplying some of the local dealers. He steals the mangoes on the way from fetching the cocaine, so that he can keep his real 'merchandise' hidden," Jordan replied with a self-satisfied smile. "And I've got it all documented right here," she said with a shake of the camera dangling round her neck.

The next series of events happened in quick succession. Mr. Cullen made a desperate lunge for the camera around her neck, half dragging the unsuspecting Jordan with him as he lumbered towards the bush. Not wanting to risk injuring Jordan, it forced the officers to lower their weapons and pursue on foot.

Ms. Elizabeth Snickles, having recovered from her intense sprint along the tarmac, charged with impressive speed to her master's aid. She sank vicious teeth into a fleshy ankle.

Mr. Cullen screamed in pain and tried to shake the furry creature off his ankle, but someone professionally trained Liz in the art of tug-of-war. The brief canine distraction enabled Jordan to shake herself, and her camera, loose from his grip and allow the armed policemen to do their job.

With Cullen safely in handcuffs, and a couple of officers counting the haul of illegal drugs, detective Turner pulled Jordan aside.

"You said you'd been working on this for a month?" he questioned her, his grey eyes softening as they stared into hers.

Jordan fought off the usual flutter of wings inside her stomach, furious with her fickle teenage girl hormones that muddled the usually simple logic of her mind.

"I know where you're going with this," Jordan replied defensively, her eyes deliberately leaving his, "but I didn't want to bother the police with something that I wasn't sure was an actual case. I only had a desperate farmer wanting to know where his mangoes were disappearing to."

"And that led to the biggest haul of cocaine this department has ever confiscated…" Turner replied seriously. "This was too close, Jordan," he said in a lowered voice, concern creasing his handsome face. "I know Natasha and I have had a lot going on at the station and we haven't had time to listen-"

"Exactly," Jordan drew away from him, "the big, secret case you've both been working on which, detective Rain made very clear, had zero room for teenagers. It's why I handled this alone. I didn't want to be any trouble."

"Regardless, today could've gone very wrong," Nicolas explained, his hand reaching for her shoulder. "How would I ever explain to your uncle -"

Natasha Rain's anxious voice interrupted their conversation. "You mentioned something going wrong. Well, something did!"

Nicolas turned to the blonde woman. She wore skin-tight black slacks that outlined the impressive curves of her muscular legs. She whipped a wave of perfectly curled blonde hair over her shoulder and pouted plump lips. Even the bulky bullet-proof vest did nothing to hinder her beauty.

"We missed them, Nick! All this waiting and planning and they slipped right through our fingers."

Nicolas turned round to face the woman. Jordan was forgotten.

"That's not possible. There hasn't even been a robbery yet!" Nicolas replied almost breathlessly. "Our source said…"

It was the first time Jordan had ever seen the composed and calm detective lose a fragment of his cool. She stepped closer, still unseen by the two adults, who seemed to tower over her and make her feel like even more of an insignificant and silly teenager.

"It happened earlier than it was supposed to. We've just received the call," Natasha replied, her shoulders slumping forward with defeat.

"Where?" Nicolas demanded.

"Jewelry store."

"How bad?"

"Bad. They got all the high value stuff."

Nicolas swiped a hand over his forehead as if he could not believe what he was hearing. He kicked out uncharacteristically at a rock on the tarmac with a polished and un-scuffed shoe.

"How did they get past us?"

Natasha's striking blue eyes flickered to Jordan's. "We were distracted. They took advantage."

Chapter 2
Settling Things Over Fish and Chips

"Thank you, officer Brown. I really appreciate you escorting Jordan home. Again."

Officer Brown scowled at Jordan, his thick eyebrows connecting in the middle, before he exited the restaurant into the warm summer evening.

The tall, scraggly man that was her uncle turned to stare at her, his lean-fingered hands sliding onto his hips. She was always struck by how his sea-blue eyes pierced through even her most defensive front. His shaggy hair framed a stern expression, which he maintained for a few seconds before his thin lips twitched into a smile, and his eyes danced with amusement.

"You're the only teenager I've ever known who gets brought home by the police because they're annoyed that she's solved a case before they even knew it existed," he said, before breaking into a grin. "Let's celebrate!"

She watched as her uncle stalked over to the bar, leant over the counter, and helped himself to the beer tap.

"I'm still too young to drink, despite my being here all of six months," Jordan reprimanded him, before handing her beer to one of their regulars who had yet to clear out for the day. "Shall we talk in your office?"

Clarence nodded at his niece before following her to his office. The smell of old wood and resin filed her nose. It was a vast improvement from the stale beer and depression that used to saturate the little room. Her uncle had changed from her time at Dandelion Drift, despite the difficulty of everything he had been through.

"So, what did you fix this time? Stolen pearls? Cheating boyfriend?" her uncle asked while slumping into his favorite ragged armchair that looked as though it may have once been a sort of palish green, before an army of cats had taken to it with sharp claws.

"No," Jordan said, pacing across the room. "This one was a little more serious."

"How much more serious? Not another dead body."

Jordan shook her head. "No, definitely not. I never plan to deal with one of those again."

"Then what? The mango farmer?"

"Yes. I found the thief. Fred Cullen?"

"The local shopkeeper who charges us a fortune for all the fresh produce we buy for the restaurant from him?"

"That's the one. Well, he's officially out of business."

"What?" her uncle bellowed in shock. "I didn't know you could go to jail for exorbitant prices."

He chuckled at his own joke for a moment before taking his foot tapping niece slightly more seriously.

"He was stealing from farmer James."

"Ah, a pity. James has had a hard time getting by with the dwindling stock he's had available."

"That's not all. Cullen was also using the mangoes to hide the drugs he was distributing to all his dealers on the island."

Her uncle slopped a considerable amount of beer into his lap, which Liz was only too happy to lap up before taking a nap on the arm of his chair.

"Anyway," Jordan continued in a hurry, "I don't have time to go into all the details now. We've got an additional problem, well, two, actually."

Her uncle closed his mouth and eyed his niece with renewed respect. He had brought her to Dandelion Drift to help him discover the figurative rat on his staff that stole from him bringing the business to its knees. This had been because he had been fully aware of her underground reputation as a teenage detective, though she referred to herself as a sloth… no, she had corrected him a dozen times… she was a sleuth. He was not sure he was comfortable with his only niece taking on drug suppliers.

"So, I figure the way to solve the first problem," Jordan had been saying, and her uncle realized he had drifted off during her anxious monologue, "is to grow our own vegetables."

"Wait, I'm lost," he said after a sip of what beer was left. He knew he should not, but he needed something to calm his nerves whenever Jordan was planning to take on the world and make it a better place.

Jordan raised an eyebrow at the near empty glass in his hand.

"I spilt most of it!" he explained, gesturing at his beer-soaked shorts.

"I've put Cullen behind bars, which means we will have to go to the mainland to source another supply of fresh food. Which got me thinking, why don't we just start our own garden? You've got the land, Uncle, and in the long run it would save you considerable cash. And you'd be able to employ a new person to work the land."

Her uncle stroked his shaggy, grey whiskers while he thought.

"I think you're onto something. The only problem is that I'm not hiring anyone extra until I can see that your idea in action is worth something."

"Fine," Jordan sighed, completely undeterred. "I'll organize it myself."

He grinned at her again. She reminded him so much of his sister, her mother.

"Stop thinking about Mom," she ordered him with a stiffness about her that seemed to hold back her own pain.

"How did you?" he spluttered in shock, nearly losing the rest of his precious beer.

"I could see the wave of sadness wash through your eyes and knew you had to be thinking of her," Jordan replied.

"Your mom had quite the green thumb," Clarence said with a fond smile, his eyes glistening.

"You had to bring her up..." Jordan broke off and wiped the involuntary tears from her own eyes.

The pair exchanged an understanding look before laughing together. The vision of each other blurred through shared tears over a mutual lost loved one.

"What was your second problem?" her uncle asked, while wiping his face clear of any residual sadness that might set his niece off.

"Oh yes," Jordan shook her head free of the memories, "I blew a major case and now the entire police station hates me."

"It can't be that bad."

"Oh, it's bad. I know Rain and Turner have been all hushed about it for some time. I snooped around the station a bit, and I knew it had to do with rumors of an infamous thief heading this way."

"The mango stealer..." her uncle guessed with a laugh.

"Not quite. This one seems to be higher end. Anyway, Natasha caught me digging around on her computer and they banned me from the station till their case was over. I'll have to use a disguise the next time I try anything like that," she half muttered to herself. "Anyway, today I found out that there was a heist at the jeweler on the mainland. They cleared the shop out."

"Marty? He must be heartbroken! Those jewels were his life's work."

"It gets worse," Jordan continued. "My little cocaine bust caused an enormous distraction and the thief got away."

"Ooh, that's not great. Don't worry," he tried to cheer up his sullen niece, "I'll offer the detectives a couple of free lunches on the house."

"I don't think your famous fish and chips are going to help me get out of this one," Jordan sighed. "I thought I was helping, but I just ended up messing things up for them. I feel like such a stupid kid."

"I don't know many stupid kids who get drugs off the street all on their own," her uncle reminded her. "And besides, if this thief is famous, that means -"

Jordan snapped her fingers and her mind immediately snapped onto her uncle's line of reasoning.

"That he's likely to strike again, and when he does, we will have another chance of catching him. I mean," she corrected herself, "the good detectives will, of course."

"Exactly, now as for you," he clapped his hands together, which awoke a sleeping Liz, "you've got chores to catch up tomorrow morning before you go off trying to catch jewelry thieves."

"Chores," Jordan groaned. "I thought my cleaning the streets of drugs might earn me a little rest."

"If you're going to insist on sneaking out at night to solve cases," her uncle fixed her with a beady eye, "yes, Jordan Parker, you're not the only one with a detective's eye, then you'll need to find a gap to rest on your own time."

Jordan giggled guiltily, feeling terrible about having misjudged her uncle's knowledge of her whereabouts.

"Sorry, Uncle," Jordan apologized before giving him a peck on the cheek. "I promise I will be more responsible and let you know where I am."

"I'd appreciate that. The real reason I want you to go about your chores is because I think some residents here might need your help with a few things."

Jordan rubbed her hands together with glee, understanding her uncle's hidden meaning precisely.

"And of course, there's this vegetable garden you've promised me," he added.

"You want me to start tomorrow?" Jordan complained.

"Hard work killed no one," he reasoned with a smirk.

"I beg to differ," Jordan laughed glumly. Her uncle had a way of reminding her she was still under his roof and ought to obey his rules.

"Now, shall we see to some dinner?"

Liz licked her lips.

"Fish and chips?" Jordan suggested.

"Can't go wrong with fish and chips."

"Yes, I agree, although a salad would go down a lot better, especially if we do baked potatoes instead of chips. Much healthier, Uncle, I agree," Jordan added with a daring smile.

Her uncle laughed, powerless to resist Jordan's whims. It was as though she intended for him to live forever. It had broken his heart when she had discovered he was a complete emotional mess after his wife had walked out on him. Alcohol had been his only numbing comfort, and he had descended the depths of an intoxicating hole too deep to escape from. Until Jordan arrived. She was only eighteen, but she bore the fierce determination her mother had once wielded, especially as she yanked him out of his hiding place from the world and forced him to become a better man for her.

Jordan had not only ousted the thieving rat running his restaurant dry, and uncovered all the stolen money, but she had also taken strict control of the budget. This meant less money on beer and more money spent on the crumbling and rotting restaurant in desperate need of attention and customers. When she had arrived, she had nearly fallen through the termite eaten deck and taken a swim with the fish in the lagoon that stretched out below his restaurant on stilts. He had to admit that with the improvements on the decking, and the restaurant itself, more customers were trickling in and things were looking up.

And that was when his stomach would pang, not only with hunger pains, but with guilt.

"What's with that look?" Jordan asked, her nose crinkling with confusion. She was aware that his thoughts were not on fish and salad anymore.

"I appreciate all you've done, Jordie," he began in a gentle voice, his blue eyes softening slightly.

Liz licked his hands, as if sensing the change in his emotions.

"Don't give me this speech again," Jordan groaned dismissively.

"You can't stay here and fix me forever. You've got your own life to live. You're still young. You don't need to be stuck here looking after an old fart like me."

"Do I?" she laughed coldly. "What life is that exactly? My father insists I study at the most prestigious university in the world, all so that he can brag about his daughter having a fancy doctorate, or something. That's not the life I want. And don't call yourself an old fart."

"What do you want in life, Jordie? That's the question we're all dying to know the answer to. You know your mother would want me to ask it."

"For now, I want to be here with you. You're the closest thing I have to my mom, so I know she would approve of my being here. And besides, I enjoy being in Dandelion Drift. The sea, this island, the people… it's exactly the change I need after being pent up in a stifling city. This feels more like home and family than the giant, cold penthouse apartment Dad put me in."

"He's doing what he thinks is best for you."

"Even you don't believe that, Uncle," she replied under her breath. "Throwing money at someone is not what's best for them."

"You need to mend things with him."

"I'd rather mend things with you. I don't want you to throw me out."

"I'd never throw my favorite niece out!" he declared.

"I'm your only niece," she laughed.

"So, fish and chips it is, then," he replied with a twinkle in his eye. "I'll cook. Your cooking is abysmal. More suitable for rabbits than humans."

Chapter 3
In the Shoes of an Amateur Sleuth

"Morning, chef," Jordan said, carrying in a box of fresh mangoes. "Farmer James sent these over for us. I thought mango ice cream might be a pleasant addition to our desert this evening."

Duncan paused, his heavy blade hovering over the heap of onions he was chopping to prepare for the day.

"Meant as a thank you, I'm sure. I heard you figured out who's been robbing farmer James blind," chef Duncan said with an approving smile. "You're quickly becoming a valued member of this community."

Jordan tapped her nose and smiled conspiratorially. "I do not know what you're talking about. How's the family?" she asked the tall, redheaded man, who looked like he could have been part of the Scottish soldiers fighting for independence.

Duncan's knife clattered loudly against the granite counter, scattering diced onion everywhere. Jordan's jaw dropped when she realized the huge, hulking chef, who had been smiling moments before, was now sobbing. His broad shoulders shook, and a flood of tears disappeared into the depths of his bright red beard.

"I'm sorry," he apologized, before blubbering even louder.

"There, there," Jordan replied awkwardly, her tiny hand patting his enormous tattooed forearm. "What's on your mind?"

"It's my Chloe," he sobbed. "I love her so much, but I just don't think she feels the same way about me anymore."

Duncan wore no wedding ring, so she had always assumed he was a bachelor. She watched as he used the corner of his apron to dry his eyes, which then teared more profusely because of the onion juice soaked into the fabric.

"Alright," Jordan led him to a chair and shoved some Kleenex his way. "Why don't I make you a quick cup of tea and you can tell me all about it?"

Jordan set about making the tea and was still trying to figure out if Chloe was a lover or a pet, when Duncan began his story.

"My Chloe is the most beautiful woman you'll ever meet. It was love at first sight, well from my side, anyhow."

"When did you meet?" Jordan asked, while setting a steaming mug down in front of him.

"High school. I followed her everywhere and finally she agreed to date me. We had so much fun," he recounted, with fresh tears soaking into his beard. "Those were the happiest times of my life."

"What changed?" Jordan inquired.

"I don't know. Things were great, but she said she needed more money, so I started working longer shifts here. She's a woman who likes to look good and look after herself. You'll get there one day. She said she had found work on the mainland too and soon we had very little time for each other."

Jordan tried to mask her discomfort at discussing budding marital problems, but she could sense a potential case coming her way, so she listened closely.

"What is it you suspect, exactly?"

"Suspect?" Duncan asked blankly.

Jordan twitched in her seat. "Well, I fear you wouldn't be talking to me, of all people, about this, unless you thought there was something I could find out for you…" Jordan drifted off, hoping Duncan would get to the point.

"You're right," he sighed, his head dropping to his arms that rested on the table. He sobbed for a solid five minutes, pausing only to bark at his assistant to continue chopping the onions and stop staring.

"I think…" he finally managed, through quivering lips, "that she might be having an affair. I've been denying it for some time now, and I couldn't bear to ask her myself, but is there a way you could… you know…"

"Say no more," Jordan reassured him in a low voice. "I'll find answers for you, though I have to warn you they might not be the kind you're hoping for."

He nodded mutely. "I understand that. Just do what you need to. I deliberately took her set of house keys with me this morning so I could make you a spare set for you. She's coming in to fetch them, so you'll see what she looks like and judge for yourself."

"I'll do my best, and," Jordan dropped her voice to a whisper, "I promise you can count on my discretion, too."

Duncan nodded appreciatively, before downing his tea and hoisting himself out of his chair. His orange Crocks squeaked on the clean kitchen tiles as he moved over to his station. He shunted his assistant out of the way and was morosely hacking his way through a bowl of onions when Jordan vacated the kitchen.

Word had certainly gotten out that she considered herself something of an amateur detective. It did not help that the police and detectives were wrapped up in their own private major case, leaving many of the locals floundering with solving their own problems.

As Jordan made her way to the breakfast room to replace the flowers in the vases, a hiss from the cleaning cupboard under the stairs caught her attention. The door was ajar, but it was dark inside and Jordan could see no one. Liz yapped with delight, so she knew it had to be someone she knew. She stepped closer, her curiosity getting the better of her, and an arm flopped out and pulled her into the cupboard under the stairs.

"What's going -"

Jordan felt a warm hand cover her mouth. She could smell disinfectant, coffee, and a faint hint of cinnamon.

"Scott?"

"How did you know it was me?" he hissed back.

"I could smell the coffee on you, so I knew it had to be one waiter who works the coffee machine."

"How come you didn't think I was Luke?"

Luke was Scott's twin brother and also a waiter at her uncle's restaurant. While the pair were almost identical physically, their personalities were vastly different.

"Your hands also smell like table cleaner. Luke never scrubs his own tables after the guests leave, so I knew it had to be you."

"You're so smart, Jordie," Scott crooned with admiration. The warmth in her voice made her a little uncomfortable about being crammed into a tiny, dark space with him.

Liz growled, a subtle sign that the young man was becoming a little too friendly with her master, whose chest was rammed up against his.

"Okay, so what's with the cupboard? You've obviously got something on your mind that you don't want anyone else to know about."

Despite keeping him at bay, Jordan liked Scott as a friend. He had always been kind from her first day, yet not invasive and borderline pervy like his twin brother, Luke. Jordan liked Scott because he seemed to see her as an actual person, rather than a silly teenage girl with a hot bod and a pair of green eyes he could hit on. Sensing Scott needed help, Jordan felt inclined to want to be there for him.

"Is it true that you figured out Tamara's boyfriend was cheating on her?"

"Yeah. Thought that didn't require rocket science to figure out."

"And you caught the guy robbing my uncle James?"

"That's right."

"What about the alien sighting?"

"That's new," Jordan snorted. "Sorry, the last one is not true."

It shocked her how quickly word of her reputation had spread throughout the small island town. Her father would be furious if he got wind of what she was using her first year out of high school for. Helping the lowly and not earning a dime. At least the table wiping and floor scrubbing paid her a minimum wage from her uncle. Dad would be *so* proud.

"Well, that's good enough for me. I need your help, Jordan, and it's really important."

"Okay, what's bothering you, Scotty?"

"You know how I've been saving for my own car?"

"Yeah."

"Well, I think someone has been stealing my tips. I know I should earn more, but every day I count up, I get less and less."

Jordan thought for a moment. "I think I know how to solve this one."

"You do?" his voice squeaked excitedly. Jordan could smell coffee on his breath, with a hint of mint.

"Who has Tamara been dating since breaking up with the other guy?"

"My brother, though she says she won't stay with him unless he gets himself a car. She's not a fan of his Vespa."

"Come with me," Jordan said with a sigh.

She dragged Scott into the light of day and straight to the tip jar at the manager's desk.

"Give him his tips back," Jordan ordered Tamara.

Tamara fixed Jordan with an icy glare. "I don't know what you're talking about," she replied obstinately.

"I know you're in charge of distributing tips at the end of the day. You've been giving Luke his brother's tips on purpose."

Scott's jaw dropped open in shock as all the obvious clues jumped into place.

"Why would I do something like that?" Tamara scoffed, though her face reddened at the lie.

"Because Luke is trying to save for a car, and if he gets one, it means you won't have to be seen on the back of his olive-green Vespa. Out of everyone here, you're the one who cares most about what people think, so I know you wouldn't mind stealing from Scott to make it easier for his brother to get a car first."

"Tammy wouldn't do that," Scott denied with love-filled eyes.

It was a known fact that both Scott and Luke had been competing for Tamara since her first shift.

"Hand it over, Tamara, or I'm getting my uncle involved. You know the policy, we're a no-thieving staff here."

Tamara scowled ferociously but obeyed. She pulled out a notebook and added a few figures together with her pencil before delivering the total amount that Luke owed Scott.

"What's worse is your brother didn't even question where the extra cash was coming from, and you're the only two waiters here."

This cold fact punched at Scott, and he took a moment to comprehend just what Jordan meant. His face dropped with sadness.

"How could you do that to me, Tam?" he asked with a croak in his throat.

"Look, I wasn't thinking about you. I just kind of wanted to help Luke. Scott, I am sorry. I'll make sure all the tips go to you, including mine, until we paid the debt."

Jordan was not expecting such a quick turnaround from Tamara. She had even detected sincerity in her voice.

"Excuse me," a voice hesitated to interrupt them. "Is it alright if I go to the kitchen?"

"Hi, Chloe," Tamara greeted the woman upon noticing her. "Yeah, Duncan is expecting you. He said something about your keys."

"Thanks, Tam, you're a lifesaver."

"Chloe, Duncan's wife?" Jordan seized the opportunity to begin her new case promptly.

"Yeah," Chloe smiled sweetly. "And you are?"

"I'm Clarence's niece, Jordan. Nice to meet you."

"Yeah, I've heard your name before. You didn't have something to do with farmer James getting his mangoes back?"

"You know what rumors are like, almost never true," Jordan answered ambiguously.

Chloe laughed. "That's what I thought when I heard about the hidden treasure map you supposedly uncovered."

Jordan had to admit that Chloe was nothing like she imagined. She was expecting a peroxided blonde, wearing a tight mini skirt, and advertising all her assets. Chloe was the exact opposite. She was dressed tastefully in an elegant dress that highlighted her huggable figure without being immodest. Her make-up looked natural and classy, and her hair was pinned up neatly, revealing her slender neck and delicate earrings that caught the morning light. It was hard to believe that a woman of such beauty had been snatched up by Duncan, however sweet his nature.

"You really can't believe half of what people say," Jordan corrected her.

"Yes, I know exactly what you mean," she chuckled. "Anyway, I'm in a bit of a hurry. Nice to meet you."

As she turned to leave, she dropped her purse. Scott, unable to help himself in the presence of such a gorgeous woman, darted forward and retrieved the purse so that Chloe did not have to bend down.

"I'm so clumsy," she giggled, her cheeks reddening slightly as she accepted the offered purse. "Thank you…" she said, her fingers slipping over his.

"Scott," he replied quickly. "And you're not clumsy. You're lovely, really."

Jordan bit down on her lip to force herself not to scream with shocked laughter at Scott. He was usually so shy, yet he had mustered up the courage to not only approach Chloe but also compliment her.

"Thank you, Scott," Chloe replied with the slightest bashful smile, before turning to leave.

Tamara and Jordan maintained their composure until Chloe was out of sight. They then erupted with both delighted and horrified squeals.

"You're lovely," Tamara copied in perfect imitation.

"What did I do wrong?"

"Nothing," Jordan laughed. "It's just that it took you an entire week before you could even look me in the eye, but after five seconds with *Duncan's wife*, you're all ready to woo her."

"I was just…" he paused, his mouth gaping open and closed like a fish out of water. "Oh my gosh, she's Duncan's wife!" he gasped. "I hit on his wife! He's going to kill me!"

Tamara snorted with delight. "You'd better do my chores for a week, or I'll tell Duncan."

"Speaking about chores," Jordan smirked. "I have a new one for you."

"What do you mean?" Tamara stammered.

"It's going to be a quiet day in the restaurant, so my uncle wants Scott to handle your position for the day. He needs to test out his managerial shoes."

"And me? I need my salary. I can't just go home!" Tamara protested in a flood of panic.

"No, he specified that you're to help me get started with the restaurant's new project. You'll still get your usual pay, and a little extra for the manual labor."

"Project?" Tamara asked, confusing creasing her heavy layer of make-up. "Manual… labor?"

Jordan tossed a pair of rubber boots and a work overall at Tamara's feet. She had donned the outfit herself and after pulling a hat down to her ears, she grinned at the disapproving Tamara.

"What are you playing at, Parker?" Tamara snarled, her arms folding across her chest.

They had gotten off on the wrong foot from the moment they had met. Tamara had taken an instant dislike to Jordan, seeing her as a threat instead of a potential friend. It did not help Jordan's friendship efforts, when Tamara ended up being one of Jordan's suspects in a murder case. They had proven her innocent, of course, but Tamara had, frequently, displayed a general lack of honesty and a desire to pocket as much money as she could. Clarence refused to fire her since he knew the family had hit hard times and needed every penny Tamara brought in.

"We're going to start a vegetable and herb patch for the restaurant. Once it's producing, there should be enough produce for the staff to take fresh vegetables home to their families."

"It's a brilliant idea," Tamara admitted to Jordan's surprise. "But you're an utter idiot if you believe that I'm going to get my nails and hands dirty digging up all of this."

The pair looked out at the weed coated patch of dirt which was filled with rusted cans, plastic bags, and dead shrubs that Jordan's aunt Rebekah had likely planted before she walked out on her family.

Jordan handed Tamara a pair of gloves and grinned again.

"Come on, Tam, it will be fun. Look, I know we're far from being friends, but I know deep down you care about the restaurant, and this is a way we can help it climb back to its former glory. And besides, it's extra pay."

Tamara yanked the gloves from Jordan's hand and glowered at her. "Don't call me Tam."

After fighting over where the boundaries for the actual garden would be, Jordan and Tamara finally settled into a good work rhythm. They began by picking up all the trash. Tamara suggested most of it could be recycled to bring in a little more cash for the seeds. Next came the tedious task of digging out all the weeds and shrubs. It was exhausting work, and the late morning humidity did not help their cause.

Jordan nearly cried with relief when her gangly uncle came out carrying a tray from Duncan. They sat in the shade of a tree and munched on fresh tuna and cucumber sandwiches, which they washed down with icy lemonade.

"You seem pretty nifty with a shovel," Jordan acknowledged, breaking the uncomfortable silence that always hovered between them.

"Yeah, well, some of us grew up working. We weren't all born to privilege like you."

"Does your family live on a farm?" Jordan asked politely, forcing herself to ignore the bite in Tamara's remark.

"No," Tamara shook her head. "Just a small patch of land on the mainland. The soil isn't as good there as it is here, but I try to grow a few things for the house."

Jordan smiled at her. "You didn't tell me you had green fingers. This project will definitely be a success with your experience."

"Why do you try so hard?" Tamara thrust the question between them, breaking all futile attempts to maintain a civil conversation. "You literally don't have to be here, so why do you pretend to care about all of us?"

"I know I don't have to be here," Jordan admitted. "I know I'm still an outsider. But this place is more like home than anywhere else."

"That makes no sense. This place is a dump, and from what I've heard, you've got your own mansion in the city, so why stick around here? You could have any pick of a university, any pick of a country you want to live in. You're wasting your time here."

"Is that how you feel about living here?"

"This isn't about me," Tamara rounded on her. She dropped her empty lemonade bottle to the ground and whipped up her gloves again.

"This may not seem like a good enough reason to you," Jordan said quietly, "but my uncle's my closest family, and I have little family. My father may have plenty of money, but he doesn't really know what's best for me, or care about what I really need. My uncle doesn't have a dime to his name, but I trust his judgement of me. I feel like when I'm around him, I can figure out where I come from and that will help me grow into who I want to be."

"Your uncle is a good man," Tamara agreed stiffly, though Jordan could see the intended kindness warm her eyes. "So, I can respect your wanting to be here with him. I guess I can kind of see your point. My family has no money, but there are tons of us and we're close. I can't imagine not having that."

It was the first time Tamara had offered her anything other than derision and scorn.

"But I still think you're a spoilt brat who doesn't belong here."

And Tamara was back to her old self, but Jordan smiled at the tiny glimmer of the inner person she had glimpsed, hidden beneath a protective shield of animosity.

They both set about digging out old roots and weeds that polluted the soil and would make it impossible for new seedlings to survive without being smothered.

"Ew," Tamara protested after removing some overgrown weeds.

"What is it?"

"An old shoe," Tamara remarked. "I mean, who goes walking out in the bushes and loses a shoe? It's just careless."

"Looks like they lost two," Jordan remarked, while digging out the toe of a second matching shoe. She flicked it out with her spade at Tamara as a joke.

Tamara screamed. Her face turned white, and her eyes rolled into the back of her head before she crumpled to the ground, as if in slow motion.

"It's just a shoe," Jordan remarked with a laugh at Tamara's overly dramatic reaction.

She crouched to inspect the offending shoe, which looked as though it had spent some time underground. Only then did she notice something else protruding out of the hole she had dug.

Jordan was next to scream.

She dropped back onto her hands and scuttled away as quickly as she could, her light green eyes fixed fearfully on a dirty human toe poking through the soil.

Chapter 4
Fingers and Toes

"Where's my tall latte?"

"Here, detective Rain," Scott said as he tripped through the upturned soil and sloshed half the coffee inches from Natasha's expensive shoes, which were already suffering from all the mud.

"Shall we try that again? This time with a full cup," Rain ordered Scott before turning away in a huff. A sure way to end up on Natasha's bad side was to mess up her coffee. "Where's the body?" she demanded, with an aura of self-importance clouding her vision.

"It's uh… in the taped off section," officer Brown replied, despite the answer to her question being visibly obvious to everyone on site.

The yellow taped off rectangle was impossible to miss. Natasha simply enjoyed the sound of her own officious voice bellowing across a scene of crime.

"And who found the body?"

"A Tamara and a…" he hesitated. "A Jordan Parker."

"Oh, jeez," Natasha groaned and threw her hands in the air. "Why is it that every time we have a body in Dandelion Drift, she's got something to do with it?"

"Maybe because I'm more capable of detecting crimes that have happened than you are?" Jordan replied with a snide smile. "Nice to see you again, Nats."

"It's detective Rain to you," Natasha replied, the skin around her jaw twitching as she clenched it.

"You must be excited, detective Rain," Jordan added with another smile. "Your second dead body in your entire detective career."

Natasha and Jordan had begun on the wrong foot upon their first meeting. They had shunted the young detective into a promotion because she was one of the few police officers able to pass the exams to become a detective. An overworked Nicolas Turner agreed to babysit her, if she agreed to the job. This had resulted in an overconfident and inexperienced detective taking charge of many of the cases Jordan longed to get her hands on.

Jordan naturally despised someone like Natasha Rain. She was, in part, jealous of Natasha's barbie doll perfection, but mostly, she was jealous of the badge Natasha wore on her hip. It was a license to justice, to finding truth, and to setting matters right in the world. In Jordan's youthful eyes, too many wore it without a shred of honor, which was why she refused to allow herself the dream of joining any kind of law enforcement. She preferred to work from the shadows, doing what she could to help.

"You know," Natasha's voice interrupted her thoughts, "it's rude to insult someone and then disappear mentally. It gives me no chance of retaliating."

Jordan realized that there was no way she could have anything to do with solving the appearance of a grizzly body in her garden unless she pandered to Natasha.

Jordan frowned at her, her lips twitching into an unnatural smile. "Sorry. Have you seen the body?"

"Not yet." There was a slight hesitation. "Care to show me?"

"What did you have for breakfast?"

"Waffles," Natasha replied without thinking. "Why?"

Jordan gestured into the neatly dug out grave. It was shallow, and the body had only been there a few months, which meant there was a lot more grisliness than just a pile of bones.

"Oh my gosh," Natasha gagged in fright as she laid eyes on the figure. She turned to hurl, but detective Turner was approaching the scene.

Unwilling to have her boss see her throwing up because of her inexperience with dead bodies, Natasha bolted for a nearby tree, losing one of her shoes.

Jordan almost felt bad when the sounds of regurgitated waffles reached her ears. She snorted with laughter, though she knew she would undergo the same humiliating process if she risked looking at the corpse in its entirety for too long. Her brief encounter with the toe had been enough to inspire nightmares for the next year. To her relief, the toe had still been attached with all the other little piggies.

"Jordan," Turner greeted her, his eyes studying hers. "Are you okay?"

"I'm better than Natasha. She's heaving out her waffles on that tree over there."

Jordan felt the slightest twinge of guilt, which she ignored, for highlighting Natasha's incompetence every chance she could.

"I remember doing the same with my first few bodies," detective Turner sympathized. "This is not pleasant work. I'm surprised you're holding up…"

"I screamed and fainted at the sight of the toe. She admitted quietly to Nicolas that she hadn't been able to view the whole body.

"I knew it, you little punk," a pale faced Natasha hissed behind her. "You're climbing down off that high horse of yours and facing this body with me. You can put that overworking and annoying brain of yours to good use."

Before Jordan could protest, Natasha had hooked an arm through hers and was pulling her back towards the shallow grave. Jordan bared her punishment with what little dignity she had remaining. She screwed her eyes shut and only opened them a fraction, so that her long, dark eyelashes would act as a censor for the horrors that lay below.

"Right, detectives," Turner began, the amusement clear in his voice, "I'd like to remind you to treat this with the respect this body deserves. This was a living person who had family and friends who had to mourn a terrible loss. Remember that when you're tempted to screech and squeal in disgust."

Natasha jutted her chin upwards, refusing to be shamed by her earlier reaction.

"Since you're both here, let's make this interesting," Turner continued. "Share your observations and whoever gets the most correct, in line with the upcoming coroner's report, will get a free dinner on me."

Turner assumed a free meal would be an adequate incentive for both ladies, while unbeknownst to him, it was actually the possibility of spending time with the handsome man himself more than anything.

"It's a woman," Natasha observed first, her eyes barely flicking to the body.

Jordan gritted her jaw and allowed herself a squint. "Middle aged. Uncared for."

"Uncared for?" Turner asked her to clarify.

"What's left of her clothes are mismatched and too big for her. The shoes she was wearing belonged to a man. This makes me think she was very poor or homeless."

"I think that puts you in the lead, Parker," Turner remarked with a smile. "Come on, Rain. Show her what proper police training can do."

"She was shot. Bullet is still lodged in the chest," Natasha squeaked before gagging again and turning her back on the body.

"Excellent," Turner applauded. "What else?"

"Broken leg injury," Natasha threw over her shoulder, "though not caused at the time of the murder. You can see the pins in the bone. I think that puts me in the lead!"

"That it does. Knowing you, you'll force me to do oysters. Come on, Parker, save me from the oysters!"

"She's wearing my aunt's ring…" Jordan stammered, her words falling out clumsily.

"Wait, what?" Natasha demanded, spinning back to stare at the body.

"How do you know that's your aunt's ring?"

"I recognize it. My uncle had it custom made for her. There should be an inscription on the inside."

"And we have a winner if the report confirms the truth of that!" Turner announced, though Jordan had forgotten entirely about their petty competition.

"Why is my aunt's ring on a murder victim's body?" she murmured to herself.

"Which aunt would that be?" Turner asked quickly.

"Rebekah Walker," Jordan replied, numb to the core. "She was married to my uncle Clarence."

"You asked what her ring is doing here…" Natasha repeated the question. "I think the answer to that question is fairly obvious, Parker. When last has anyone seen or heard from your aunt?"

Jordan turned slowly to face the smirking detective.

"You're not arresting my uncle again!" Jordan informed her between gritted teeth.

"I have to!" Natasha said back, her voice edging up a few octaves. "His wife's ring is on the finger of an unidentifiable *female* victim. What are we supposed to conclude?"

"I don't know!" Jordan confessed. "This is all too bizarre."

"How old do you reckon this corpse is, boss?" Natasha asked Turner.

"My guess would be around six months."

"And how long ago did you aunt leave?" Natasha demanded from Jordan.

Jordan refused to answer the question. It was a coincidence. There was no way her uncle would lay a finger on her aunt Beca. It was not in his emotional or physical vocabulary to hurt her. Natasha's bombarding questions and her towering height were oppressive.

"I'm afraid we will need to take your uncle Clarence in for questioning. They found the body on his property and the connection to the coroner will easily disprove your aunt if it's not her," Turner offered with his most reassuring smile.

Jordan shook her head, backed away from them, and turned to run. She had to warn her uncle. If Natasha delivered the news that his ex-wife's wedding ring had been found on a body in his garden, it would push him over the edge. Jordan had to get there first.

She dodged the bumbling officer Brown and ran straight for the restaurant. She heard Turner instruct them to leave her alone, and knew he was allowing her the kindness of informing her loved one first, before Natasha rained down on him.

Chapter 5
Find Anything on the Internet

"So, we're back here again," Natasha began, her painted fingernails drumming against the old table.

"I'm thinking you've developed a crush on me," Clarence replied dryly. "Or are you just trying to get back at my niece for always upstaging you in your own cases?"

"This is not personal, Clarence," Nicolas informed him. "Just a few routine questions." He was sitting in to make sure it was not personal.

"Then you're not trying to prove I killed my ex-wife and buried her in the garden?"

"If the shoe fits…" Natasha remarked. "No one has seen or heard of your wife since her last visit to Dandelion Drift to collect some personal items. This was the day they finalized your divorce. Correct?"

"Correct."

"And even when your son passed away earlier this year, there was no sight or sound of his mother at the funeral. Odd, don't you think?"

"Not really," Clarence replied, though he visibly steeled himself against the affronting memories. "Beca walked out on all of us without looking back for a second. I don't think she cares about us anymore, whether we're dead or alive."

"Reports from people who know you claim that you've been drunk ever since she left," Natasha continued ruthlessly. "Drinking away your guilt, possibly?"

Detective Turner cleared his throat and seemed to take a deliberate sip of his coffee, as if to send an unspoken message to his inexperienced partner.

"It's alright, detective Turner," Clarence addressed him after noticing the exchange. "Let the young woman do her job. I know what I am… or should I say, what I was. A drunkard -"

The telephone on the wall buzzed, cutting Clarence off. Natasha was too busy staring down Clarence to even notice the phone, so Nicolas left his seat and answered the call.

"I wasn't aware Mr. Walker had requested a lawyer," Turner said into the phone.

"What are you playing at?" Natasha fired, her eyes never leaving Clarence. "There's no way you could afford a lawyer."

"I don't know what you're talking about," Clarence replied innocently, though his blue eyes twinkled mischievously.

"Mr. Walker does not want a lawyer," Natasha barked at her boss.

Nicolas raised an eyebrow at the lower-ranking detective, as if to remind her of her place.

"Well, if the lawyer is insistent that she was called for," Turner was saying.

"Oh, right," Clarence slapped a hand to his forehead and chuckled, "I remember now. I *called* my lawyer."

Natasha's piercing eyes narrowed dangerously. She could sense something was off, but could not put her manicured finger on it.

"You haven't even had your one phone call yet," Natasha reminded him, her brow creased with suspicion.

"I texted her." Clarence shrugged with a grin.

Turner sighed in the corner, his endless supply of patience rapidly running dry. "Just send the lawyer in, so we can get on with things," he instructed the officer on the other end of the call.

Natasha growled with disapproval. She downed her mug of coffee, her eyes never leaving Clarence throughout the duration of her noisy slurps.

Minutes later, the door burst open, and a woman strode confidently in wearing a pair of elegant black heels. She wore a pin-striped pencil skirt, with a white button up collared shirt, and a thin black tie.

"Nice shoes," Natasha mumbled before she could stop herself.

The woman, with neatly pinned up brown hair, smiled faintly at them with striking red lips, her intense green eyes emboldened by the make-up she wore. The young lawyer slammed her leather briefcase onto the wobbly table and dragged a steel chair next to Clarence, where she seated herself.

"My name is Jordan Parker and I'll be representing my uncle," the woman introduced herself, without the trace of a smile.

Clarence buried his face in his hand and cracked up, laughing behind it. Nicolas Turner allowed a smile to broach his lips, too, as he slowly recognized the familiar woman who had disguised her youthful self with too much make-up and a superbly fitting business suit.

"You!" Natasha all but screamed. "What are you doing here?"

"I'm representing my uncle," Jordan repeated herself. "My documents are all in order, if you'd like to check."

"I would like to check!"

Jordan pulled a printed page out of her briefcase and handed it to Natasha to peruse.

"This isn't real," Natasha said, casting it aside without a single glance. "You're eighteen. There's no way you got through law school."

"The online website which charged me a dollar fifty assured me they were legitimate," Jordan replied with a smirk.

Natasha looked as though she was about to go down for murder.

"Okay, okay," Turner said, laying a calming hand on Natasha's forearm as she reached for her empty gun holster. "You obviously went to a lot of trouble to be here with your uncle, so we might as well hear what you have to say."

"Thank you, detective Turner. I have nothing to say yet, so please, detective Rain, continue your interrogation of Mr. Walker. I will be here to advise my client."

Natasha rolled her eyes. "You've got to be kidding me."

"Detective Rain had just pointed out that I've been a drunkard for the last six months or so and that they haven't been able to locate your aunty Beca."

"Thanks for filling me in."

"My point was," Natasha growled, "that if you'd been inebriated since your wife left you, then it's quite possible that, upon her return to fetch the last of her belongings, you shot her in anger."

"Why would I kill the only woman I've ever loved?" Clarence asked, his voice cracking.

"You were furious about the divorce going through. You weren't in your right mind, wrought with grief and sozzled by alcohol. And then, upon sobering up, you panicked and buried her in her own vegetable garden. But before you did that, you slipped on her wedding ring, ensuring she would be no one else's again."

"That's quite a detailed theory," Nicolas pointed out.

Jordan raised a finger so that she could politely interrupt.

"Excuse the intrusion into your carefully thought-out piece of fiction, but if my uncle was inebriated at the time of killing his wife, then how did he shoot so precisely?"

"What?"

"The bullet was lodged in the center of the victim's chest, proving it was someone with trained shooting experience. My uncle has no such training, and they knew him in the community to be a peaceable man who does not like weapons. Had you asked the people you interviewed more than, 'does he drink?' you would've discovered that yourself."

Natasha glowered at her. "It's likely it was a lucky shot!"

"Then where's the gun? There is no licensed gun in my uncle's name. And one more thing," Jordan interrupted again, "if my uncle was sober when he buried his ex-wife, surely, he would've been smart enough to *remove* her wedding ring, the same ring he had designed and engraved for her. Unless he wanted to get caught…"

"Then how was the ring on her finger?" Natasha demanded.

"Uncle, would you care to explain what happened to my aunt's wedding ring?"

"After she left for the last time, I went up to our room to… process what happened. It broke my heart when I found she had left her ring on my pillow. I knew then that there was no hope of us ever getting back together. I couldn't bear to see it anymore, so I tossed it out the window in a fit of rage. It must have disappeared into the field where we found the body."

"And what, slipped onto a corpse's finger? How convenient."

"I'm not so sure, detectives, that the corpse we found today really is my aunt," Jordan continued, ignoring Natasha's protests.

"That's ridiculous -"

"Let her explain," Turner interrupted. "We are still waiting for the coroner to confirm the identity, though I'm interested in hearing your findings, Jordan."

"For a start, my aunt was nearly six feet tall. I had to look up some old photographs before coming in, but as you can see clearly," Jordan spread several photographs across the tabletop, "Rebekah was far taller than the body we found today."

"In case you hadn't noticed, there was a distinct lack of flesh on today's body, which affects the height."

"Jordan has a point, though. Looking at the photographs from the grave, the body we found had a shorter bone structure compared to the lanky woman in the pictures we see here," Turner agreed.

"I also took it upon myself to call the Walker family doctor," Jordan continued, while pulling out another piece of paper.

"Can I see that?" Natasha interrupted her before snatching the paper from Jordan's hand. "These are chemistry notes. What are you playing at, kid?"

"Turn it over," Jordan urged, though her cheeks reddened from the embarrassment of recording her notes on a scrap page from her science workbook. "You will see the transcribed conversation I had with Doctor Wallace."

Natasha reluctantly flipped the page and struggled to make out Jordan's untidy scrawl.

"You can call him yourself. He will explain that my aunt had two sound legs which had never experienced a breakage of any kind, and had no pins from an operation," Jordan announced with triumph as she slammed her fist on the table for theatrical effect.

"Ah," Turner said with a smile, his own brain cogs churning.

"There's one more thing," Jordan added. "My aunt had impeccable teeth, in fact, she had all her own teeth. The corpse we found today was missing several front teeth."

"Let me guess," Natasha retorted sourly. "You called your aunt's dentist."

"I can have dental x-rays from her records emailed over in minutes, if you'd like," Jordan replied with a self-satisfied smirk.

"I believe that's an extra ten points for Parker," Turner concluded after draining the last of the coffee. "Shall we get going?"

"What?" Natasha exploded. "She's slowing down our investigation right now, not earning points!"

"On the contrary," Turner corrected the scarlet faced Natasha. "The young sleuth is speeding up our investigation. She has proven, using resources available to her, that her uncle is innocent of murdering his ex-wife, simply because the woman buried on his property is *not* his ex-wife."

"Then how did the ring get on her finger?" Natasha complained. "I will not rest until I know Rebekah Walker is still alive!"

"Perhaps if we figure out the identity of our Jane Doe, we will better understand why she was wearing my aunt's ring," Jordan answered.

"There is no *we*," Natasha hissed at her. "There's the police and then there's you being weird. Stop meddling in affairs you don't understand and let the adults deal with the case."

"On the contrary, detective Rain, I believe you owe my niece a thank you," Clarence interrupted, his voice low and his gentle face summoning firmness.

Natasha gulped air and blinked rapidly at her exonerated suspect.

Jordan shook her head and said, "It's unnecessary, Uncle. Let's just get you home."

"It is absolutely necessary," he insisted. "You run around this town making the lives of our respectable policemen and women far easier, and you receive none of the credit." Clarence turned back to face Natasha. "In just over an hour, my teenage niece discovered enough evidence to move your case forward. You may see it as interfering, but if it weren't for her, you'd still be stuck here badgering me into confessing to a crime I didn't commit. Now, detective Rain," Clarence rose quickly from the victim's chair, "swallow your pride and go figure out who's lying in our morgue!"

It was not like her uncle to speak up against anyone. Jordan's face flushed, and she felt hot tears spring to her eyes. She tried to wipe them with the back of her hand and caught Turner's eye, quietly observing her. She lowered her gaze to her lap while her hands blindly shoved all her fake documents back into her briefcase.

"You're free to go, Mr. Walker. And as for you, Jordan," Nicolas turned to her, "thank you for the work you've done behind the scenes. Of course, we will need to confirm your investigative findings, but you've given us some solid leads. Thank you."

Natasha mumbled something inaudible, too, but she averted her eyes. Jordan found she did not really care what the detective thought. She followed her uncle out of the interrogation room and numbly out the station, feeling as though everyone was staring at the little kid in ridiculous high heels and clothes too old for her.

"You'd better drive," Jordan announced after tossing her uncle the keys to his truck.

"Then how did you get here?" her uncle stammered as he stared at his truck parked askew over two spaces.

"Well, technically, I don't have my license, but I needed to get around quick. There are a few new scrapes, but I figured if I broke you out of jail, you wouldn't mind so much," Jordan answered with a grin.

Clarence chuckled, though his face went slack when he noticed his truck no longer had side mirrors or taillights.

"You were spectacular in there, Jordie," her uncle commended her again. "I've never been so proud of you in all my life."

Jordan found the tears returning, and she hid her face in the palms of her hands. The grown-up make-up and clothes were no longer enough to hide the little girl's heart she wore on her sleeve.

"What's wrong?" Clarence asked as he gruffly pulled her into a hug. "Look, I know it's been a tough day for you, what with finding a body and all, and then the fear that I'd murdered your aunt —"

"I never believed that for a second!" Jordan sobbed, mascara streaking her rouged cheeks black. She clung to his hug, drawing in the smell of everything that was her uncle. The stale beer was a distant scent, but the clean soap smell, mingled with the natural fragrance of his skin, took her right back to her childhood. When her cousin had been bullying her, and her aunt was too busy to intervene, her uncle was always the one to pick her up and bandage her wounds. He did this while elaborating on a joke he could not remember the punchline for, but which was still hilarious nonetheless. He reminded her so much of her own mother.

"I know, I know. There, there," he soothed, patting her awkwardly on the back. "I'm sorry if I embarrassed you in front of your detective friends."

"Natasha is not my friend," Jordan snapped. "And you didn't embarrass me."

"Then why the tears?" he asked, swiping a finger across her cheek.

Jordan drew away from him and wiped her face. Her uncle could not bear the silence.

"Did I upset you?" he begged.

"Not at all."

"Then what's wrong?"

"I've… I've had no one stand up for me like that," Jordan mumbled before jumping into the truck.

Her uncle walked round to the driver's seat and climbed in next to her, though he did not start the engine.

"What do you mean? I know your mom would've stood up for you."

"That's true. She did when I was a kid," Jordan agreed. "But she's been gone for some time and somehow life got a lot more serious after that. My dad always assumed I was in the wrong. He hates the idea of his daughter being an interfering sleuth nosing in people's affairs. If he had any idea what was going on…"

"That's why you refuse any credit," her uncle said with understanding in his voice. "I don't want you to feel ashamed of who you are. You did a good thing today, and that Natasha cop was only all salty because you showed her up in front of her boss."

"I didn't mean to," Jordan whispered. "Okay, I did a little, but I also just want her to see that I can be of help. I'm tired of being treated like a kid."

"Being a kid is not such a bad thing. Maybe you should try to enjoy what's left of your teenage years before rushing into adulthood. Once you're here, there's no going back. And fixing my life, and my restaurant, shouldn't hang on your shoulders."

"Don't start that again," Jordan shook her head.

There was a tap on the glass that startled them both. Jordan swung round to find a gloomy Natasha at her window. She lowered the glass and stared at her nemesis.

"I'm sorry for jumping to conclusions and not considering the evidence like you did," Natasha managed in a strangled voice.

"Is Turner holding a gun to your head?" Jordan joked to ease the strangeness of having Natasha apologize to her.

"No, but he dropped my score to zero after I threw a tantrum in the interrogation room," Natasha complained. "Your uncle is right, though. I lost sight of the case because of my pride."

Jordan found herself speechless, which was a seriously rare occurrence.

"Anyway, we need to figure out who that body belongs to before we can find the killer. Would you..." Natasha studied her painted fingernails, then she adjusted her hair, before finally settling her crystal gaze back on Jordan. "Would you like to come with me?"

"Is Turner forcing you to do this?"

"He says we make a good team."

"That's ridiculous," Jordan laughed dismissively.

"That's what I said," Natasha sighed. "But he claims our mutually competitive spirit helps push each other to new heights... or something like that. Anyway, are you coming or not?"

"She's going," Clarence answered, before his niece's pride got the better of her. He leaned over and pulled the door handle. "Be home before dark."

Chapter 6
Poor Jane Doe

"So, although your uncle acted like a complete butt towards me, what he did was kind of cool," Natasha admitted quietly. "I didn't really take him for the type to stand up to two detectives and set them in their place."

"Uncle Clarence is the calmest and most peaceful person I've ever known. I think he's seen too much sadness in his life to waste time getting angry or mean with others. But there's also a quiet strength buried beneath the shaggy exterior, which most people overlook."

"I can see that now. I felt like my father was scolding me," Natasha said with a guilty laugh. "And he was right to. I just get so involved in a case, and so hellbent on a theory, that I lose sight of the woods for the trees."

"I know what you mean," Jordan agreed shyly. It was the first genuine conversation she had embarked on with Natasha where there were no insults, screaming, or arrests.

"Where are your parents?"

"Mom's dead. Dad's overseas, somewhere far away, I hope," Jordan replied in a voice deliberately void of emotion.

"Ah."

"Ah?"

"That explains your insanely tight connection to your uncle. This is the second case we've had where you've leapt to his defense without doubting him for a second."

Jordan did not feel like delving into too much depth with Natasha, just because the detective was deciding to be nice. She also did not feel like being profiled, if that was the real reason for the rival detective dropping her mean act.

"What about you?" Jordan diverted the subject.

Natasha pulled up at an old wooden café. A little boy dressed in an oversized beach shirt ran up to her.

"Hey Nats," the kid greeted her with a twitch of his bushy eyebrows.

"Don't call me that. One tall latte and a...?"

"Chocolate milkshake," Jordan opted, taking advantage of the paying detective.

Natasha pulled another bill out of her purse and handed it to the kid.

"Thanks, Tommy," Natasha said as the rough-looking kid darted inside the café.

"Isn't he too young to work here?"

"He doesn't work, really. He's got no family and won't stay in the system. I try to help a little, giving him odd jobs. He fetches coffees for cops, so they don't have to get out of their vehicles while on the duty. He's also had quite a few titbits of information that's proven handy."

Jordan realized there was far more to the blonde bombshell in stilettos and a shirt with a plunging neckline than she initially thought.

"Anyway, you asked about my family. Only child, with great parents who have always pushed me to do my best."

"Lucky," Jordan remarked.

Having such a stable family background explained Natasha's immense confidence in blowing through life as it hit her. She never had to waste time second guessing herself, though Jordan thought it might prove more beneficial if she did.

"Here are your drinks," Tommy announced as he slipped the takeaway cups through the window.

"Thanks, Tom, keep the change."

Tommy flashed a grateful grin through chapped lips and pocketed the coins which jingled with his other earnings.

"Any news for me on the street about the jewelry store heist?" Natasha said, after lowering her voice.

Tommy shook his head. "Things are quiet. Too quiet. I don't think the thief has moved any of his stolen goods yet. He must be waiting for the heat to die down or else he knows more people on the street than I do and is keeping them quiet."

"What about the body found on the island? Heard anything about that?"

"Can't say I have, but I'll put word out. How old is the body?"

Jordan thought this a strange question for an eleven-year-old boy to be asking, but then she realized she had been asking similar questions far younger. She looked at Tommy with new eyes. He was no longer just a street urchin, but a kindred spirit in the amateur sleuth world.

"Right now, we're still trying to figure out who our victim is," Natasha explained. "But the body is about six months old.

"I'll keep my ears open," Tommy promised, though Jordan noticed that a tiny wave of shock passed through his face.

"Thanks, kid," Natasha winked at him.

"Any time, Nats," Tommy waved at her and blew a spontaneous kiss before darting away to help another patrol vehicle that had just pulled up.

"Is it just me, or did he seem to know more?" Jordan inquired.

"Maybe. He likes to check his facts before talking to me."

"I think we should offer him a milkshake and see what else he can remember," Jordan suggested.

"He will talk when he knows something, okay? Hold on, I'm getting a call." Natasha rifled through her handbag. She sloshed hot coffee down her leg in the process and between her screeching and the blast of her Katy Perry ringtone, Jordan could feel headache developing.

"Hello? Great. I'll be there now," Natasha confirmed.

"Who was that?"

"Turner. The coroner has an identity on our victim."

"How did they figure it out?"

"I guess we will find out."

"Thanks for coming all this way. Our local doctor never would've been able to handle this one for us," Turner was saying to the city doctor, who had travelled out to their humble precinct to assist with the case.

Jordan eyed the young man. He had a healthy head of fiery hair barely tucked beneath his medical cap. His eyes were a warm green, and he smiled readily. She offered him a shy wave, but he barely noticed her. Jordan turned to see who or what the young coroner was staring out and saw Natasha pulling her blonde locks up into a ponytail.

"Hi, detective Rain," the coroner greeted in a shaky voice. "Good to see you again."

"Have we met?" Natasha asked blankly.

"It's Ray," Nicolas replied quickly. "He's from the city. He comes through for the troublesome cases. Doctor Bentley, this is Jordan. She's a sort of consultant for our small team out in the sticks here and has proved a real asset."

"Nice to meet you, Jordan," Ray greeted her. "I hear the pair of you were quite accurate with your diagnosis of the victim. She was middle-aged, short, and had suffered a broken leg damaged so badly she needed pins to help set the bone. She died of a gunshot to the chest, which caused a rib to puncture the heart and she bled out in seconds. And she is not Rebekah Walker if I look at the structure and dental records."

Jordan aimed an 'I told you so' smile at Natasha, who ignored her.

"I think that makes Jordan the official winner of the dinner," Turner announced to a beaming Jordan and a downcast Natasha. "But I'm sure Ray would appreciate if you escorted him to dinner? You could show him how much fun we can have on our little island."

The coroner grinned at Natasha with obvious excitement while she looked as though she would rather be dead, like their chilled victim hiding under a clean sheet.

"Right, enough of that," Turner continued. "The identity."

"Ah, well, I traced the serial codes on the titanium rods used in her leg. They were registered to a public hospital where a Ms. Rosanna Smith was treated almost ten years ago. I also cross-checked this with DNA I could pull from hair follicles on the victim, and it matched Rosanna Smith."

"So, the victim's name popped up on the police database?" Jordan asked quickly.

"Exactly. There was a criminal record from about thirty years back. Petty theft, but the owner pressed charges. Her name pinged a second time under the missing persons register. Rosanna went missing six months ago."

"Now we know why," Natasha mumbled.

"Missing from where? Someone must have reported her missing," Jordan pointed out.

"We tried contacting the name and number left by whoever made the report and soon discovered they made it up. When I asked the officer who handled the paperwork for the missing person's case, he said a group of homeless people had come in and reported Rosanna missing."

"Explains why nothing was ever done about it," Natasha shrugged.

"Why would anyone want her dead?" Jordan mumbled.

"Wrong place at the wrong time," Natasha shrugged. "We can hand it over to officer Brown to do interviews among the homeless."

"Why officer Brown?" Jordan asked again, confused by Natasha's sudden lack of interest in the case.

"Let's take this outside," Turner suggested. "Thanks for the hard work, Dr. Bentley. If you find anything else, please get in touch."

"See you for dinner later, Natasha," he called as Natasha stormed out of the room.

"What's up with you?"

"This case is a bust," Natasha sighed.

"But we finally know who our victim is," Jordan countered.

"Exactly," Natasha groaned. "Look, when it's a homeless person… things kind of take a slower pace."

"That's fair," Jordan retorted sarcastically. "Rosanna had her life taken from her."

"It's not that she's less important, it's just that there is no family pressing us to solve this. There's no immediate killer on the loose. We can take our time while other more pressing cases take priority."

"Like?" Jordan snapped, her cheeks hot.

"Like the robbery of the town's biggest jewelry store and the threat of another future heist. This is a small town that can't afford to sustain losses like that, so we need to give it priority while it's still a threat to our economy," Turner explained rationally.

Jordan felt nauseous in the pit of her stomach. She could understand the reasoning behind the two detectives needing to slow down on the murder case, but it still did not feel right to her. Why was money more important than a lost life?

"We can talk more about it over dinner, Jordan," Turner informed her with a weak smile. "You got the most things correct on the coroner's report, so I owe you dinner. Remember?"

"Yeah, I'll see you later, then," Jordan mumbled. "I think I'll walk home."

"In those shoes?" Natasha asked doubtfully.

Jordan kicked them off and shoved them in her bag before turning to leave. She needed the alone time to think about the case.

Chapter 7
Between the Daisies

"I'm not so sure I like the idea of you going to dinner with Nicolas Turner," Clarence objected.

"Don't make it weird," Jordan protested.

Though she had raided her aunt's cupboard that afternoon for her lawyer's clothes, she was not about to do the same for a date with the detective. She did, however, have a floral summer dress on that cut just above the knee. Not that her uncle could see much of it because Liz was curled up in Jordan's lap. Jordan stroked her hand down the length of the noodled body.

The poor dog had suffered major separation anxiety. Jordan had had to lock Ms. Snickles at home because the police department would have seen through her disguise if the familiar white fox-dog was at her side, with twitching black nose and pointy ears. And her aunt had not possessed a handbag large enough to hide the dog in her entirety.

"What if he makes a move on you?" Clarence continued, his hand on his hip.

Jordan beheld her uncle. He was hard to take seriously when he was wearing a pink apron smeared with bright red pasta sauce.

"He will not make a move on me," Jordan sighed.

"But I've cooked and everything," he complained and gestured to the pot of bubbling bolognaise sauce. "You'd turn all of this down for some fancy meal at *another* restaurant?"

"I appreciate that," Jordan said with a smile, "but I already promised detective Turner I'd go to dinner with him. It's my reward, after all."

"Is Natasha going to be there?"

"Not exactly," Jordan replied, her cheeks turning pink.

"So, it's a date?" he blasted at her.

"Date? Did I hear date?" Scott repeated as he waltzed into the kitchen to fetch more ketchup. "Chef says he's out."

"It's not a date," Jordan insisted. "He's like way older than me. And if it makes you feel any better, Liz will be with me."

The little dog yawned and stretched in response to hearing her name mentioned in conversation. Her nose twitched at the tantalizing scents in the kitchen.

"Girls with daddy issues are often attracted to men older than them," Tamara pointed out. She stepped out of the pantry and grinned at Jordan.

"Look, there's nothing going on between Nicolas and me. It's a professional dinner, that's all."

"Then why are your cheeks so red?" Tamara teased.

"If things don't work out with big, impressive Mr. Cop, do you think you'd like to go on a date with me?" Scott asked timidly.

"No dating amongst the staff!" Clarence boomed.

"Sorry, Mr. Walker!" Scott quavered. "I'll just be on my way."

Jordan's phone broke out in Elvis Presley's *Jailhouse Rock,* and she looked down to see 'Nicolas Turner' calling.

"Oh my gosh, he's like calling you!" Tamara squealed.

"How did he get your number?" Clarence growled again.

"Everyone, just calm down, okay?" Jordan shouted. "Hello, detective."

Jordan's ear was blasted with endless sirens in the background and in that moment, before the detective said a word, she knew dinner was off.

"I have to cancel our plans," he began. *"I'm so sorry, but there's been another robbery. The bank alarm was triggered minutes ago and we're fearing the worst."*

"Please, don't waste another second apologizing. Just do what you need to get done," Jordan assured him.

"Thanks for understanding," Turner managed before cutting the call.

"It's off. They've got a case pop up."

Jordan ignored her uncle, who was wiping imaginary sweat off his forehead. He pulled out another bowl for Jordan.

"Joining us, Tam?" her uncle asked politely, his hand reaching up for a third bowl.

"If you don't mind," Tamara accepted shyly.

Tamara had been a little different since the day they had discovered the body together. She had not exactly been warm and friendly, but she had certainly been less hostile.

"Is it anything to do with the body we found?" Tamara asked.

Jordan was a little surprised that Tamara was starting a conversation with her, and no insult had been flung her way.

"Uh… no," Jordan replied. "They've put that case on hold."

"What?" Tamara stated in genuine shock. "But why?"

"They uncovered the identity of the body. Turns out it was not my aunt, as they first believed, but a missing person. Rosanna Smith."

"Old Rosanna," Clarence repeated. "She was one of the homeless. I just assumed she vacated to another town when I didn't see her around collecting tins out of the trash cans in town."

"No, sadly, the real reason she disappeared was she was shot and then dumped in your garden."

Clarence slumped into a chair, his face grim.

"But why are they putting the case on hold?" Tamara asked.

"Officer Brown is taking over the investigation for now. The detectives explained that it's not a top priority anymore, and they have to focus on their other more pressing cases."

Tamara scowled viciously, though for once she did not direct her disapproval at Jordan.

"But you're going to carry on the investigation yourself, right?" Tamara demanded more than asked.

Jordan thought while twirling spaghetti onto her fork. She did not really know what to do. Officer Brown loathed her even more than Natasha did, and Jordan suspected that if he caught her snooping around the case, he would not hesitate to throw her in a cell and leave her there to rot.

"I mean, it's what you do, isn't it?" Tamara asked faintly. "You solve things."

"I'm supposed to. But I've also got another case I haven't even touched," Jordan admitted. The mention of chef Duncan had reminded her she still had to look into the question of his gorgeous wife's fidelity.

Tamara glared at her while slurping up a forkful of tomato spaghetti strands. Jordan could not shake the feeling that she had somehow disappointed her.

"The pasta is good, thanks Uncle," Jordan said gratefully. "Since I'm not going out with detective Turner anymore, do you think I could borrow your truck, one last time, to check out something important?"

"What kind of something important?" he asked, his blue eyes fixing on her.

Before Jordan could answer, the door to her uncle's private kitchen swung open. Liz sounded a warning growl as a woman stepped in. The woman wheeled a small luggage bag behind her, which seemed to carry more airline stickers than clothing.

"I heard you killed me," the woman stated in a deep throated voice that sounded as though it belonged on a country album. She had intended her opening line to create a dramatic effect.

"Who's that?" Tamara asked.

"Aunt Beca?" Jordan stammered uncertainly.

"Jordie," her aunt cooed affectionately. "Well, don't just sit there with your pasta falling off your fork. Come give your aunt a hug."

Jordan obeyed, though every muscle in her body felt stiff.

"Rebekah, what are you doing here?" Clarence asked tentatively. He avoided her gaze.

"I couldn't ignore my favorite niece now, could I," Rebekah replied.

"What is she talking about?" Clarence asked.

"I may have emailed Rebekah to ask her to contact the police and prove she was still alive. I didn't realize she'd fly halfway round the world and come here."

Clarence closed his gaping mouth, picked up his pasta bowl, heaped a few more spoons of saucy noodles on top, and disappeared out of the room as though Rebekah Walker did not exist.

***

Jordan glanced up at the starry sky and felt grateful that there was no moon. She needed the cover of darkness if she was going to snoop around unnoticed, though it would make catching anything on camera more difficult. She flinched at the crunch of gravel under foot, aware that every sound was infinitely louder at nighttime.

Jordan pulled out her uncle's truck keys and unlocked the door as quietly as she could.

"That's called stealing, you know," a voice accused out of the darkness.

"Tamara!" Jordan gasped in fright. "What the heck are you doing out here? I thought you went home hours ago."

"I knew you'd be up to something," Tamara hissed at her, the whites of her eyes glinting in the night.

"Technically, I asked my uncle if I could use his truck," Jordan reminded her.

"Yeah, and then your aunt walked in and stole the show. Your uncle never had a chance to reject you."

"How do you know he would've?"

"Because you don't have a license."

"I did the test a few times, okay, so I know how it all works."

"You actually have to pass the test," Tamara pointed out.

She snatched the keys from Jordan's hand and slipped into the driver's seat.

"You coming?" Tamara asked.

Jordan hesitated again. She did not know whether Tamara was being seriously cool, by not ratting her out, or if she was planning to make use of the recently emptied grave in her uncle's vegetable garden. Liz seemed to trust her and was already sitting happily on the passenger's seat.

"I have a license," Tamara assured her. "I'll drive, as long as you let me come with."

Loud voices from her uncle's office drifted over to them. Arguing.

"Look, jump in. Neither of us wants to get caught up in that," Tamara cautioned.

"You don't even know where I'm going," Jordan protested, though she climbed into the passenger seat.

"I'm sure it has something to do with the little old lady's case," Tamara guessed after revving the engine to life.

"I wish it did," Jordan said sadly. "But I promised a friend I'd give his case top priority tonight. Is that why you wanted to come with, to find out who killed Rosanna?"

"Kind of. I haven't been able to get it out of my mind. Like, who just shoots a person and then shoves them in a hole in the ground?" Tamara complained, while the truck jerked into third gear.

"I thought you said you had a license," Jordan accused her.

"I do. I've just had nothing to drive before."

"Look, it's never easy seeing something like that. I've been struggling to get those images out of my head, too. It's why I wanted to find Rosanna's murderer, because then my mind can finally relax, knowing that she's received some kind of belated justice."

"Exactly," Tamara agreed, her hand thumping against the steering wheel. "Jeez," she laughed, "I never thought you and I would see eye to eye."

"I just don't really know how to carry on the case, you know, since the cops pulled out."

"The Jordan I've gotten to know doesn't really care what the cops are doing. You just go right on ahead and fix things yourself. Where do you get your drive from?"

"Cat!" Jordan squealed in fright, her hand bracing against the dashboard as a ginger cat darted across their headlights and narrowly missed the front tires.

Tamara swerved and mounted the curb for a few seconds, but the cat lived to roam the streets for another day.

"Sorry, I'm also a little night blind, but it's fine, really."

Jordan buckled her safety belt and said a silent prayer before answering Tamara. "I don't know. I've always been like this. I'd always figure out if someone pinched my sweets when I was a kid, or if my dad had smoked again on the sly. It kind of just grew from there. And the more I developed it, the more it irritated my father, so of course I had to keep sleuthing," Jordan laughed.

"I'm kind of…" Tamara hesitated. "Kind of jealous. You've got so much that excites you in life. So much potential. You're one of those people who can do anything you set your mind to."

"Yeah, well, I kind of envy you," Jordan admitted.

"No, that's not even possible."

"Apart from the fact that you're so super confident around guys, and I'm a bumbling ditz, you've got incredible motive to get done all you do."

"That's ridiculous. And all I do is scrub tables and hand people their food."

"Yeah, but you stick it out so that you can support your family. You don't get it, because you've always had it. But you come from a close family where you'd do anything for each other. I wish I had that as my motivation."

"You've got close family too…" Tamara replied awkwardly, though Jordan could hear she was struggling to speak past the lump in her throat.

"Do you mean a father who doesn't call anymore because I refused to go to college, or a cousin who died trying to murder me, or an aunt who travels halfway across the world to scream at my uncle and forgets she hurt me too."

"But you've got Clarence," Tamara interrupted her pity party. "Quality over quantity."

This silenced Jordan. She had been so busy complaining about who she did not have that it had momentarily slipped her mind that she had someone who cared deeply about her, and who had the same mischievous twinkle in his eye as her mother did.

"And as for the boy thing, Scott has been dying to ask you out. You're just always too distracted to notice."

"He's a little young for me," Jordan remarked. She turned her face to the window so that Tamara would not feel the heat radiating off her cheeks.

"He's like three years older than you," Tamara laughed. "Just give him a shot."

"You stole his tips from him!"

"I wanted him to learn to stand up for himself. Luke pushes him around constantly. He has to grow up."

The truck skidding to a halt in front of a house interrupted their conversation. Jordan clambered onto the dashboard.

"Sorry, I'm not used to these brakes. Here's chef Duncan's house," Tamara announced.

"Gosh, we're right in front. Can't you scoot forward so we're not so obvious?"

Tamara turned the key to start the engine again and after a few stalls and shudders that set half the neighborhood's dogs barking, they finally jerked out of sight.

Jordan was practically in the truck's footwell, keeping out of sight.

"First rule about sleuthing is you have to be more subtle!" Jordan hissed at her inexperienced and uninvited partner. "Let's cruise around the neighborhood and hide in the bushes, so we're less obvious, and then we'll proceed on foot."

Ten minutes later, they were cramped in a bush opposite Duncan's house. Despite Duncan still being at the restaurant, preparing for a small function to be held the following morning, the lights at his house were on, and piano music drifted through an open window.

The minutes ticked by and still nothing happened. There were no obvious signs or sounds of an affair taking place.

"I thought this would be slightly more exciting."

"Yeah, it takes time," Jordan replied, defensive of her hobby.

A few more endless minutes ticked by before Tamara started fidgeting again.

"What now?" Jordan hissed at her.

"Something's crawling on my leg."

Jordan used the light of her phone screen to see what was wrong, and discovered an enormous, hairy spider chilling merrily on Tamara's bare calf. She did not want to risk the inevitable screams that would ensue if Tamara spotted the beast using her leg as a resting place, so without a word, Jordan flicked the uninvited guest into a nearby bush.

"What was it?"

"Just a leaf," Jordan lied, though her lips twitched into a smile.

"What are we here for, exactly? Is Duncan worried his wife is up to something?" Tamara guessed.

As if in answer to her well-timed question, a man's laugh guffawed out the window.

"Stay back and stay out of sight," Jordan instructed in a whisper. "I'm going to try get closer."

Jordan hopped over the low picket fence, her camera slung round her neck and secured with one hand. She dropped into a bed of daisies, the white petals tickling her cheek. Liz gave her a fright by squeezing through the pickets and settling down at her side.

She could hear a man's voice, followed by a woman giggling. The second rule of being a sleuth was not to jump to conclusions, but to make calculated deductions based on gathered evidence. In simple terms, the situation could be completely innocent. It was likely not innocent, but Jordan would never forgive herself if a false report caused an ended marriage.

Jordan's calves ached from squatting for too long and Liz Snickles snored gently, her long nose nestled into her bushy cream tail. Jordan ignored the millions of mosquitoes that buzzed round her ears, making it impossible to overhear any of the low-voiced conversation taking place.

The loud cracking noises of twigs and scuffling sounds from the across the street meant Tamara was rapidly tiring of her job as lookout, and would soon attract attention from more than just the local bats and spiders.

A glance at her watch told her that chef Duncan would finish up at the restaurant soon, and be on his way home, so if there was something going on between Chloe and her mysterious male guest, who giggled almost as much as she did, then they would need to break things up soon.

She readied her camera, her fingers sweating in anticipation of what she might capture. The front door creaked slowly open, and two shadows crept out of the house, closing the door behind them. Liz jerked awake, a low snort escaping her muzzle as she protested at having fallen asleep on the job. Jordan rested a reassuring hand on her dog's head so that Liz would not give them away.

There was not enough light to capture any good pictures. Jordan turned the exposure to manual and snapped a few silent shots from between the daisies. The woman was definitely Chloe. She recognized Chloe by the shapely silhouette her perfect figure created in the darkness. The voice also matched. Chloe laughed at something and swept her long hair over her shoulder, causing something on her chest to glint briefly in the dim starlight.

Jordan grabbed a few more pictures, but unless the chatting couple embraced, she had no proof. The man had his back to her the entire time, but she could tell he was tall and had a strong build.

"If your pool pump gives you problems again, you just give me a shout," the man said in a deep voice. "Have a good evening."

And then he was gone. It was either a completely public cover up for the affair taking place behind closed doors, or the young man, who did not so much as glance backwards as he walked down the street, was simply offering his services as a pool handyman. At ten at night.

Jordan waited for Chloe to return indoors before she scampered back over the fence with Liz close behind her.

"Get to the truck, quick," she hissed at Tamara.

"Why?"

"What handyman walks to his clients? He obviously did not park in front of the house for a reason. If we can find his vehicle, then we might figure out his identity."

"I see," Tamara grinned with approval. "You're not half bad at all this."

"Thanks," Jordan laughed.

They hurried up the road towards where her uncle's truck was hidden, and found officer Brown leaning against the driver's door, with his arms folded across his chest.

"I had a feeling I'd find you here," he droned at her, his eyebrows crossing dangerously in the center.

"Officer Brown," Jordan chirped as cheerfully as she could, "what brings you out here so late at night?"

"I'm the one asking the questions," he reprimanded her immediately. "Your uncle reported his truck missing an hour ago."

Jordan's heart sank. The last thing she wanted to do was cause her uncle more stress, especially when he was already having to deal with the furious return of his ex-wife. Her disappointment rose when the taillight of a white truck disappeared round the corner. It was too far away to read the registration plate, but as the truck passed under a streetlight, Jordan caught the word 'service' printed on the back.

"As you can see, it's just a simple misunderstanding. I asked him if I could use it -"

"I doubt he'd agree. You don't have a license," Brown informed her with a smug sneer forming in the crook of his mouth.

"But I do," Tamara interrupted. She pulled out her purse and handed over the license. "It's all in order. I'm her designated driver while Jordan runs her errands."

"What errands?" Brown barked, dissatisfied that Tamara's license was actually legitimate.

"Chef Duncan asked us to check on his wife, since she's home alone, and he has a late shift," Jordan explained. Technically, it was not a lie.

"He sent two young *girls* to protect his wife?" Brown scoffed. "Now I've heard it all. You know one day, Parker, all your snooping around is going to get you caught in a rather nasty trap."

"Let's hope you'll be around to save me when that happens, officer," Jordan grinned. "Sorry to drag you out of bed for no reason, but we will head home now. I'll let my uncle know it was all a misunderstanding."

"On the contrary," Brown mumbled, "I think I'll escort you both, and explain just where I found you."

Things would not have been too terrible had Tamara not accidentally backed up into the front fender of the police vehicle, waiting to follow them. The damage was minimal, but it served as a stupendous sign that Tamara and Jordan were not fit to be driving.

Chapter 8
Unusual Partnerships

"Where do you think you're going?" a voice snapped at her from behind.

Jordan spun around and found her aunt with one hand on her hip and tapping her foot. Liz growled with disapproval.

"Beca," Jordan gulped. "Tamara and I were just heading out to -"

"You've both got work."

"Scott is covering my shift," Tamara explained. "Clarence wants him to get trained as a manager."

"Surely you need to be around to do the actual training, then?"

"I did that this morning," Tamara explained quickly, her gaze dropping to the floor.

"What about you? Surely you don't expect to live here for free?" she demanded of her niece.

Jordan bit her tongue. Of all the things she could throw at her aunt. For example, her aunt did not have any legal rights to a single wooden timber of the restaurant, as she had already received a handsome payout from her ex-husband.

"*Uncle* Clarence assigned me to work on the vegetable garden this morning," Jordan replied rigidly. "Which I did. So, I'm taking the next two hours for lunch because it's too hot to work in the field. Besides, they still blocked half the field off with police tape."

"You're working in my old vegetable patch," Rebekah repeated, her features warming slightly at the fond memory.

"No, I'm working in my *uncle's* old vegetable patch," Jordan retorted, unable to prevent her innate teenage sassiness from springing to the surface.

Ms. Elizabeth Snickles was immediately on guard. She cautiously sniffed round Rebekah's ankles while trying to decide if there was a reason for her master's hostility or not.

Her aunt's face hardened again, and she pursed her lips. Jordan could feel the tension radiating between them, and Tamara was fidgeting awkwardly. Liz was licking at her ankle, a sure sign that the dog was trying to calm her down too.

"And since when did it become okay for you to talk to your aunt so disrespectfully?" Rebekah demanded of her, her hands flicking onto her hips. "If your mother knew the police had brought home you last night, she'd turn in her grave!"

This stance would have terrified Jordan when she was a child and knew she was in for a spanking. But she felt she had outgrown that respectful reverence. She felt her lips part and form words she tried desperately not to say. Her vocal chords vibrated in her throat and the attack launched out at a person she had once loved dearly.

"It became okay when *you* walked out of our lives without a second glance backwards. 'Aunt' is a title that is *not* your right anymore because you walked away from it. If you want the respect, you once had from me, then you need to earn it. If you don't believe me, ask the man who claims to be my father. He's endured this speech too. And don't you ever talk to me about my mother again. She would have agreed with every word I've said if she lived to see you smash her brother's heart to a million pieces."

With that Jordan turned and stomped out of the room with Liz close at her heels. Tamara followed quickly too, leaving Rebekah defeated and alone in the center of the room.

"You shouldn't speak to her like that," her uncle scolded Jordan gently. He was waiting for her on the bottom step leading up to the restaurant.

Jordan sighed. It had felt terrible thrashing her aunt with words, but also tremendously satisfying at the same time.

"I'm sorry. I just got so angry when I saw her," Jordan mumbled. "She's been gone for ages, without so much as a word to tell us she's alive. And she has the nerve to tell me I should work!"

"She's not as used to having the police bring you home as I am," her uncle teased. "It gave her a fright, and she fears you're out of control. Officer Brown looked furious last night. Where were you again?"

"Working a case. This one is confidential, I'm afraid, because it involves someone here at the restaurant. But I wasn't doing anything illegal, just trying to get some pictures," Jordan explained.

"I think I know who needs your help," her uncle said, tapping his nose. "Anyway, you do all you can to help him with his situation. That little minx of his may be beautiful, but I don't trust her one bit," he said in a low voice so that only she could hear.

Jordan nodded. She trusted her uncle's judgement. He looked at her seriously for a moment, a million thoughts traveling behind his blue eyes, and then he smiled.

"You've done a good job weeding the soil so far," her uncle commended her. "But I would like you to work on your aunt."

"All she does is scream at you since she came back," Jordan snapped.

"Rebekah came back to show the police she was still alive, so that they would drop their case against me. She came at her own cost and on her own time. And, I'd like to remind you, she came because *you* wrote to her. I can guarantee you she wouldn't have done that for me."

"It's called an email these days."

Her uncle waved his hand as if dismissing her technical terminology.

"Beca's here now, and if you don't try to work on what's still left between you, then she may not return the next time you really need her. We don't exactly have a ton of family members left to pick from, so you might as well hold on to what you still have."

Jordan nodded slowly, her uncle's words seeping in and churning feelings of guilt. Her thoughts went to Tamara, who did everything for her close-knit family. But perhaps that was the reason she was so close to them. She worked on her relationships.

"I'll work on it, I promise," she agreed, a new resolution settling in her mind, scattering the dust that had clouded up the space in herself she had reserved for family.

"Great. Now where can I give you girls a lift to, since you're both officially banned from driving my truck for the next month, at least."

***

"We'll take two chocolate milkshakes," Jordan asked politely. "Actually, kid, make that three, and a small bowl of water."

Tamara watched dubiously as Tommy ran off with a fistful of Jordan's cash.

"I doubt he's coming back," Tamara snorted. "I caught that kid with his hand in my bag last year trying to steal every dime I had."

"He'll come back," Jordan replied confidently.

"What are we doing here, anyway?" Tamara asked, an edge in her voice.

"I told you. We're trying to figure out what happened to Rossana Smith."

"And you think that little kid is going to tell us something we don't know?"

Jordan was not sure. Tommy had held back from telling Natasha everything he knew. She was not sure he would open up to her, a complete stranger, and with no real money to offer him.

"Here we go," Tommy said, handing over the three chocolate milkshakes on a tray he had borrowed from the little café. "There are chairs inside if you want to sit down."

Jordan took the bowl of water off the tray and put it down for Liz, who lapped at it gratefully. She gestured to the remaining milkshake on the tray.

"That one's for you, and we're perfectly happy outside, under the tree," Jordan said with a smile.

Tommy gratefully accepted the double thick chocolate milkshake. He took a long sip, his cheeks denting inwards from the force of sucking.

"Does this mean you want information?" Tommy asked knowingly, his eyes twinkling with mischief.

"Tommy, did you know anyone called Rosanna Smith?"

The little boy froze. His eyes widened with fright, and he slowly lowered the milkshake cup.

"She was your friend, wasn't she?" Jordan added quickly before the kid bolted.

"How did you know?" he stammered and took a step backwards. She was going to lose him.

"Sorry, I'm being rude," Jordan said with a wide smile. "I didn't introduce you to one of my most important friends."

Tamara smiled in expectation, but Jordan stooped and picked up her long, white dog with fox ears and a twitching snout.

"This is Ms. Elizabeth Snickles. She wasn't with me the day I met you. You can pet her."

Tommy looked a little timid, but he raised his hand slowly and allowed Liz to sniff him. Then he dropped it onto her creamy white head and smoothed down her fur. Her brown eyes closed happily and a pink tongue darted out and licked his cheek.

Tommy giggled and wiped his cheek quickly.

"I think she likes you," Jordan laughed. "Or she's trying to get at your chocolate milkshake."

Jordan's warning came too late, and Liz's long tongue had already wrapped round the straw. Tommy jerked it away from her and erupted in an infectious giggle.

"Natasha asked you about a six-month-old body and you gave her almost the same reaction you gave me. I promise that you're not in trouble," Jordan assured him with a warm smile.

Tamara crouched down in front of him, so that she was more eye level with him.

"We just want to figure out who killed your friend," Tamara explained gently, "because we were the ones who found her, and we don't think it was right for her to be forgotten, like she's not important. We need your help, Tommy."

Tamara, having siblings of her own, was more used to dealing with kids.

"Rosie was my friend, and she was the best. She was so friendly and kind to me. She loved to drink purple colored juice though," Tommy explained sadly and with a crinkle of his nose.

Jordan wondered if the purple juice was alcohol, but she said nothing.

"Did Rosie get into some kind of trouble?" Tamara asked.

Tommy frowned slightly while he thought. "Rosie used to collect tins around town. She didn't steal like some others. But one day, after being in town, Rosie came back all scared."

"Was she hurt?"

"No, but I could see in her eyes that she was terrified."

"Did she tell you why?"

"Rosie said that she met a terrible man, and she saw him doing a bad thing. I told her to go to the police."

"Did she go?" Jordan asked.

Tommy nodded, but a scowl darkened his little face. "The police did nothing to help. When you're one of us," he jabbed dirty thumbs at his chest, "no one takes you seriously."

Jordan chewed on her lip for a second. She knew why the cops had ignored a semi-batty lady with a half-bottle of booze in her coat pocket, but it broke her heart to think a murder could have been prevented had the authorities just listened to her plea.

She dropped to her haunches next to Tamara and looked up into Tommy's sad eyes. Liz licked at his hand.

"I'm sorry they didn't listen to her. Is that why you didn't want to tell Natasha about it?"

He nodded glumly.

"Natasha really cares about you, Tom," Jordan explained kindly. "I know she would listen to you if you needed help. And I don't think she was among the cops who ignored your friend."

Jordan was not so sure about the last part. The detective had walked away from the case the second she heard the victim was a homeless person, but Tommy did not need to know that. He needed to believe in the system if he was ever going to have a safe life inside of it.

"What happened after Rosie went to the police?"

"She packed up her things to move out of town but, before she could, she disappeared. I never saw her again. I thought she had left, but then I found all her stuff still packed. She never came back."

"I'm sorry this happened to your friend Tommy," Jordan said sincerely. "I promise we will do all we can to catch whoever did this to her."

Tommy sucked at his milkshake noisily while he decided whether Jordan was really on his side, or simply another adult making promises that would fail him.

"Oh, and one other thing," Jordan added with a smile. "Liz and I may need your help again with another minor project of mine."

Tommy grinned at her. "Just find me here and I'll come help, Ms. Jordan."

"You can call me Jordie," she said, extending a hand to shake his. "Thanks for your help. I hope I can be a friend you can count on, Tommy."

A car pulled up and honked its horn, likely for Tommy. Jordan glanced over and saw Natasha glaring out her window at them.

"Hey, Nats," Jordan called, trying to shake the awkwardness of being found talking to her rival's informant.

"Why are you talking to him?" she demanded, her face contorted with suspicion.

"Just checking he's okay. He lost a friend, after all. What are you doing here?"

Natasha frowned with confusion, before redirecting her thoughts to the more immediate problem. "They hit the bank at closing time. Same guy as the jewelry store and the post office. He's making a mockery of us! I need to know if Tommy has heard anything on the streets."

"He's all yours. Make sure you listen closely. He sees you as a friend and I'd hate for you to disappoint him."

Natasha stared at her blankly. Jordan did not have time to explain. She knew where she needed to go next.

***

Jordan forced her widest smile. Liz was clutched under her arm so that she could not chew through her lead and bite someone. The police station was not the little dog's favorite place, and she had snapped at several imposing fingers in the past.

"Officer Brown," Jordan said cheerfully, while her smile wavered slightly.

Brown's eyes rolled and his grumpy face visibly dropped even further.

"What do you want, Parker?" he growled and regarded her, and her little dog, with the deepest suspicion.

"I wanted to apologize," Jordan replied sincerely. "I know I've made your job a lot harder since I've been in town."

His eyes nearly bulged out of his head as he hauled out a stack of paperwork he had had to fill in because of Jordan's existence. He rattled off a long list of her crimes, and even Liz did not escape his walk down memory lane while he pointed out the scars on his fingers.

"Look," Jordan forced another weak smile, "I know. And I'm sorry. Last night's accident -"

"You mean, when your friend intentionally rammed into my car?"

"Yes, the *accident*. It made me realize that my actions have consequences. So, I put together a little something to show how sincerely sorry I am."

His eyebrow darted up, and she could tell he did not believe her for a second.

"What are you up to?"

"Nothing!" she protested with her most innocent face.

"I don't believe you."

"Look, I left the gift on the hood of your car. It was supposed to be a surprise, but I'm betting someone steals it, since apparently there's an uncatchable thief in town."

"Hilarious," he glowered at her. "I don't know what kind of prank you have planned."

"No prank!" Jordan said, raising one free hand. Liz copied her and raised a paw. "If it helps, I'll wait right here, and you can see for yourself."

He slammed his half-full mug of coffee down.

"Not a chance. I know you're up to something. You're coming with me, and if you're wasting my time, you're going to spend the rest of this beautiful beach afternoon in a holding cell."

"Okay," Jordan stammered. "I can tell you're not used to receiving gifts."

"Shut up, Parker," he barked at her, evoking a snarl from Liz. "Lead the way."

While they made their way to the exit, a person in a heavy raincoat pushed past them, bumping Jordan and Liz into the jumpy officer.

"Watch it," he shouted at the odd person retrieving a few scattered documents he had dropped on the floor.

Jordan led him outside to his patrol car, parked out front. True to her word, there was a wrapped gift on the hood. He circled his vehicle three times, expecting some kind of surprise attack. He even checked underneath the car.

"It's not rigged or anything. Just open it," Jordan said with an impatient sigh.

"You open it," the officer insisted, while standing back.

It did not help that Liz lifted her leg against his front tire, which resulted in another glower from the agitated officer, who kept checking his watch.

Jordan pulled off the giant pink bow and slowly began undoing the polka dot wrapping paper.

"Just rip it!" he erupted behind her, unable to contain his frustration any longer.

Jordan obeyed and removed the paper. It was a box.

"Open it!" he ordered, his hand hovering over his gun holster.

Jordan rolled her eyes again and lifted the lid. She waved her hand over the opening of the box to show that nothing was going to leap out and bite her.

The officer frowned at the box but stepped closer and guardedly took a peek.

"Is this an orchid?" he gasped.

"I thought your desk could do with a little brightening up," Jordan explained. "And you look like you have a green thumb."

"How did you know?" he gushed.

"I saw how you were eyeing the various plants in the field where we dug out the body. Only a person with gardening experience would even notice what was hiding under all those weeds."

"I've got to give it to you, Parker. You're one observant girl."

"There's more," Jordan invited him to continue.

He pulled out an enormous jar of chocolates.

"I thought those could help get you through the quiet afternoons," she explained. "And there's some excellent coffee in there, too."

"Why are you being nice?"

"I'm not a bad person. Well, at least *I* don't think I am. I really do just want to help people, and even though I go about it the wrong way…"

"You mean illegally."

"Not quite, but anyway, I think I can make a difference. This gift is a peace offering."

Brown's lips twitched into an almost smile and he shook his head in disbelief.

"I really thought there was going to be a snake in here."

"I also want this to serve as an apology for the future times I'm going to step on your toes," Jordan added.

"What do you mean?" he asked sharply.

The rain coated figure walked past them on the sidewalk, whistling loudly. Liz barked and started following the person.

"I mean I don't plan on changing my ways. I'm an amateur sleuth that is going to be around to annoy you for some time yet, but I do hope we can become friends despite that," Jordan said in a hurry.

Liz was tugging at the corner of the rain jacket and the wearer was trying to shove her away with a foot.

Officer Brown sighed wearily but extended a hand to shake Jordan's.

"Thank you for this gesture. You're not half bad, Parker."

She blushed slightly as she shook his hand.

"And one more thing," she added, "I know my way home, so no more police escorts, okay?"

Brown shook his head and marched back into the station, his potted orchid under one arm.

Jordan skipped along to catch Liz before the little dog blew their cover completely. The rain coated figure turned to her and grinned.

"Does that smile mean you got what we needed?" Jordan asked in a low voice.

"Mmhmm," came the elated reply. "You should have seen me. I was like a ninja. I rolled under the counter when no one was looking, dropped the coat, and looked like another office worker from the back, while I rifled through the filing cabinet."

"What did you find?"

"There was only one statement made by a Rosanna Smith, so it was easy to make a copy, climb back into this thing, and get out of there."

"You're pretty amazing at all this," Jordan commended her new friend. "There's no way I could've pulled that file without you."

Tamara laughed. "I have to admit, hanging out with you has been kind of fun. When I first saw you, I never would've expected we'd have anything in common, or that we'd end up trying to catch a killer together."

"Well, I wouldn't have thought those manicured nails of yours would know how to dig a vegetable bed!"

Chapter 9
The Brain Huddle

Jordan sat in the center of her bedroom floor, surrounded by what felt like a web of random clues that failed to connect. Her brain hurt, and Liz's gentle snores did not help her mind to stay active.

On her right lay developed prints from her shots at Duncan's house. As she had suspected, there were no clear shots of the mystery man's face, and nothing to prove there was an affair taking place. Duncan could not identify the shadow of a man either, increasing his frustration. Jordan's camera had picked up a glint of something rather large hanging round Chloe's neck, which Duncan said he did not recognize as any of the jewelry he had bought her.

The ensuing assumptions had led him on a violent rampage through the kitchen. Pots and pans had clattered against the floor, and a lasagna had to be scraped off the wall, much to her aunt's disgust. It had taken Jordan some time to calm him down and remind him that the photographs were inconclusive, and she needed time to gather more evidence. That his wife was wearing a new piece of jewelry was not proof enough that she was cheating on him.

Duncan had demanded that she figure out who the man was. Which would be easier to accomplish if she could give his case her sole attention. The Rosanna Smith case was not going any better.

She realized how difficult detective Rain and Turner had it. She had judged them for not prioritizing a murder case, when they also had a series of heists to deal with, which was costing the town millions. Jordan sighed and dropped her head to her mattress, closing her eyes for just a moment.

She awoke, dazed and with something tickling against her cheek. She opened her eyes and stared up into the dark cavities of her little dog's nose while she licked at her face.

"How long was I asleep for?" she mumbled while rubbing sleep out of her eyes.

She picked up the photograph she had snapped of the mystery man and studied it, while racking her brain for any clues she may have missed.

"Pool pump…" she repeated vaguely. "What if that was his cover because he really works with pools? His truck had the word 'service' on the back."

Liz tilted her head as if she was trying to understand Jordan. Jordan pulled out her mobile and began a google search for all the pool services in Dandelion Drift and the mainland. Three popped up, and she jotted down the names. Jordan knew what came next.

She pulled out her laptop and searched for each business name. After wading through various newspaper archives and advertisements, Jordan could slowly work out that two of the three owner's names, along with the accompanying pictures, were far too old to be the mystery man. His voice had been young and his stance strong.

She searched for the business name. A yawn escaped her mouth and made her eyes water. Liz had given up on the case and was snoring soundly again.

The third pool company was relatively new, she gathered, because it had almost no information or history connected to it. There were no photographs of the owner, but she found a phone number listed. It was a lead, which was reward enough for her to get some sleep.

Rosanna's file caught her eye, and she groaned. She understood why the detectives had to focus on one case at a time. It was destroying her brain, trying to crack both. Jordan sighed. She knew she had reached her limit and would need to ask for police help the following morning.

Liz tugged gently at the sleeve of her t-shirt and Jordan obediently crept into bed, allowing her puzzled mind to drift off into a restless sleep.

Chapter 10
Three Birds With Two Brains

After securing a day's leave from work, Jordan began the long walk across the bridge to the mainland, admiring the turquoise lagoon teaming with early morning bird-life. Liz ran up and down sections of the bridge, barking at the birds, as if their fluttering existence was a personal offence.

"I know you got little sleep," Jordan chastised the furry creature, "but you don't have to take it out on the birds."

A familiar car pulling up next to her interrupted Jordan's conversation with Liz. The tinted window dropped, and detective Natasha Rain smiled at her, though her eyes were hidden behind dark glasses.

"Coffee?" she offered.

"Yes please," Jordan begged.

"Hop in."

Jordan did. Rain rode to the end of the bridge and turned round so that they were travelling back to the mainland.

"Weren't you going to the island?" Jordan asked, confused.

"I was," Rain replied stiffly. "I was coming to find you."

"Me! Why?"

"Well, am I disturbing your morning?"

"No, I was actually on my way to see you," Jordan admitted.

"Why?"

Jordan tried to blow out her pride with a heavy sigh. "I need your help with a couple of cases."

"A couple?" Natasha gasped. "You've been busy without us."

"Why did you want me?" Jordan returned to her initial question.

"Same reason, actually. I'm stumped with the heists, and I thought maybe if I switch to the Rosanna Smith case, I'll kick start my brain again."

Jordan laughed. "I guess we're better at solving cases together than apart."

"Oh please," Natasha snorted. "I just thought you might enjoy the morning out with me."

"Well, you can drop me off here, then," Jordan said, calling the detective's bluff.

"No, no, I'd prefer you stick with me. I really need your brain today," Natasha admitted with trace of humility.

"To your office then," Jordan directed, wind blasting through the car so that Liz could stick her head out the window and bark at the offending birds.

"I also wanted to ask why you got Brown a potted plant, and don't feed me the whole 'apology' story."

"That part was true," Jordan said defensively. "But it was also so we could steal this."

She held up the statement from Rosanna Smith.

"Okay, I'm going to ignore the theft part and bite. What's the statement about?"

"Rosanna, who, the record states, was inebriated at the time, claims she witnessed a robbery."

"When?"

"Around the same time as her death. She says she was collecting tins around the post office when she spotted a figure climb out the back window carrying a gym bag. He locked eyes with her for a second and then disappeared into the bush."

"Did you say the post office?"

"Yeah."

"Six months ago?"

"More or less."

"Does she describe the man?"

The urgency in Natasha's voice suggested Rosanna's statement was connecting a lot of dots.

"She said he was tall and had brown or blonde hair and was wearing clothes."

"Okay…" Natasha sighed. "That's not very helpful. Your theory?"

"I think Rosanna witnessed a crime. The guy must have seen her try to report it at the police station and so he silenced her. Who would miss a homeless woman, right?"

"I agree. But there's more to it. The thief we've been chasing…" Natasha reminded her, "we discovered that his first heist was not the jewelry store, like we initially thought."

"What do you mean?"

"The first heist was actually six months ago. He used it as a test run. The guy was obviously casing our town, testing how long police response took and all that."

"But if the police knew they had robbed the post office, why didn't anyone take Rosanna more seriously?"

Natasha cleared her throat and clicked her neck. "Because we didn't know they had robbed it exactly…" she muttered.

"Wait… what?"

"We didn't know the post office had been robbed until much later. It's not exactly busy, and the postmaster didn't realize a bunch of cash had been swiped, until he wanted to make a deposit… three months later."

"Oh wow," Jordan laughed. "No wonder the thief has been making easy pickings of our town."

"Darn it!" Natasha slammed her hand into her steering wheel. "He's making a fool out of me!"

"At least we know that your thief and Rosanna's killer are potentially the same person," Jordan pointed out. "So, instead of chasing two criminals, we have one to catch, but with two sets of clues to help us."

Natasha smiled. "That is a positive way to look at it. What about your other case?"

Jordan sighed. "Don't laugh, but I'm trying to figure out who my friend's wife is having an affair with."

Natasha hooted with laughter. "So, you crack two enormous cases for me, but are struggling with a small PI case?"

"Don't judge!" Jordan moaned. "I just need your help to trace this number. Once I have a name, I can see if he's my guy."

Natasha pulled over and put a call through to the office. Officer Brown complied most efficiently, since Jordan was not the one asking.

"Barry Burges."

"Can you run a quick background on him?" Natasha asked.

"Says he's dead," Brown replied on speaker.

"Dead! That can't be right," Jordan objected. "What if it's a stolen identity?"

Brown sighed audibly into the phone. "Why is Parker with you?"

"Never mind," Natasha said. "Is there an address or anything for this guy?"

"He somehow is registered to run a pool business fifty years after his death. There's an address for the business."

***

"Maybe there is more than one Barry Burges in the world," Jordan reasoned. "Or he swiped an identity and registered the business as a cover for seducing married women."

"You're so dramatic," Natasha droned.

They were sitting on a bench, sipping coffee across the road from the little pool shop.

"Stop looking so suspicious," Natasha complained.

"I'm reading a newspaper," Jordan objected.

"Exactly. You're nineteen, not ninety," she pointed out. "You should be on scrolling through your phone or snapping selfies instead."

Jordan groaned and tossed the paper aside. As she did this, a white truck pulled up across the street. It had the words 'pool service' painted on the side and back. A tall, handsome man climbed out and began unloading boxes from the back of his truck.

"Is that the same guy?" Natasha asked.

Jordan handed Natasha the photographs she had taken.

"His shape matches the outline of the man I photographed -"

Natasha gasped, her one hand grabbing at Jordan's arm.

"Ouch!" Jordan complained. "He's not that good looking. Get a grip."

"The necklace!" Natasha squeaked. "I would know that diamond anywhere."

"I thought it was a pendant −" Jordan stopped herself. "How do you know the necklace?"

"They stole it from the jewelry store!"

Jordan turned back to the muscular man, calmly unloading pool chemicals from his truck.

"Nats," Jordan hissed, "since when do pool chemicals come in small, cardboard boxes."

"They don't," Natasha said, while reaching for her phone. "Just stay calm and don't act suspicious."

Jordan gasped in shock again.

"I said don't act suspicious!" Natasha scolded her.

Jordan was hiding behind her newspaper and nodding her head toward a gorgeous woman that had just stepped out of the shop.

"That's the cheating wife, Chloe," Jordan whispered in a strangled voice.

"You've got to be kidding me," Natasha stated in flat disbelief. "There's no way they're all connected."

"So, what's the plan now?" Jordan squeaked with excitement.

"We wait for backup. Sit still."

"That's not how it works in the movies."

"This is not the movies. This is real life. We don't want to die in real life, so we wait for backup."

"But you have a gun."

"Should I remind you that Barry killed a woman? What do you think he's going to do to you, if he gets hold of you?"

"Wait…" Jordan said slowly. "Why is Barry loading his truck up again? He carried the brown boxes inside, and now he's loading them back. Though if you look closely, he's sweating a lot more."

"Because they're heavier. He's planning to make his getaway!" Natasha said, following up with several curse words. "Where is Turner? We're going to lose this guy after months of tracking him!"

"I have an idea," Jordan stated with a growing grin. "I'll distract him, and you see what's on the back of that truck."

Natasha watched in horror as Jordan darted across the road.

"Hey, Chloe!" she called as she jogged over.

Chloe stopped, her porcelain face frozen in shock as Jordan approached.

"I did not know this was where you worked. Duncan said you had a new job."

Chloe composed herself and smiled. "Jordan, right? Look, hun, I'm a little busy loading up stock for a new pool. I don't really have time to chit chat."

"I'm actually here for Mr. Burges," Jordan said as the hulking man stepped out of the shop carrying a heavy box. "I wanted to ask for a quote on a new swimming pool. My uncle is thinking of adding one to the restaurant."

Liz was jumping up against the man's leg, trying to sniff at the box he was holding.

"I'm not taking on any new clients at the moment," the man replied gruffly before trying to push past.

Unfortunately, his feet got entangled in Liz's lead and he lost his balance, dropping the box. It landed with a crunch and split open on the side. A diamond bracelet leaked out and blinked brightly at them in the sunlight.

"Well, I guess that answers all my questions," Jordan said hurriedly. She could tell by the crazed look on Barry's face that she was in danger. She turned to run.

"We have to go, now!" the man screamed at Chloe, who ran to the passenger door and pulled it open.

Barry wrapped a powerful hand around Jordan's arm and dragged her backwards. Liz went wild and tried to bite him, but a single kick silenced her. Jordan started screaming in rage until a backhand silenced her, too. She felt her body grow slack as all her power escaped. Her head throbbed where he had smacked her and she could not stop the powerful arms pushing her into the truck.

"Get in!" he yelled.

Chloe clambered in next to Jordan. Her face pale and panicked.

"We've got another witness!" Chloe shrieked at him. "They'll catch us this time, for sure."

Jordan felt a trickle of blood against her cheek and realized it was her own.

"We'll deal with it," Barry was saying. "We just have to get out of here before cops show up."

Chloe scoffed. "Oh please. Just like you dealt with it last time? You don't have the stomach for murder. I always have to clean up your mess."

"Shut up!" he shouted at her. "I told you the gun would trace back to me, so they'd never have reason to suspect you. It was the only way."

"Yeah, and then they dug her up, anyway!" Chloe hissed back at Barry.

He was struggling to get the keys out of his pocket. Finally, he shoved them into the ignition and turned the key.

"It was you," Jordan whispered, tears filling her eyes. "Both of you."

She waited for the roar of the engine to drag her away from her quaint life in Dandelion Drift, but it never came.

"Why won't it start?" Chloe demanded. "Try again!"

"It's dead!" he shouted in panic.

As Barry jumped out to inspect the engine, he looked down the barrel of Natasha Rain's gun.

"Hands in the air," she ordered him.

Chloe made a reach for Jordan to use her as a hostage, but felt the icy touch of metal against her own neck.

"Not so fast," detective Turner's voice sounded. "Climb out slowly with your hands behind your head," he instructed her.

"You okay in there, Jordie?" Natasha called her by her nickname.

"Yeah," Jordan coughed. "Just a bump to the head." She thought she'd close her eyes for just a second.

"Not so fast," Brown's voice soothed her. "Keep those eyes open, you little thief. I knew you'd get caught in a mess," he scolded her gently.

Jordan felt the grumpy officer help her out of the truck.

"I knew you'd save me when it counted," she joked. "Where's Liz?" she asked, the panic returning.

Chapter 11
Many Hands and Paws

Liz had recovered faster than her master. While Jordan was seated on a reclining chair in the shade, Liz was darting around chasing lizards.

"Where do you want the banana trees?" Clarence called over to her.

"On the outer edge," Jordan explained. "Just follow the designs I drew."

"These 'designs' are on the back of a napkin and make little sense," her aunt pointed out.

"You know this land better than anyone," Jordan said with a smile, "so why don't you stick around and help us out, Aunt?"

"I know what you're doing, Jordie," her aunt moaned at her. "Bananas over there. They will get more sun."

Jordan accepted the chilled lemonade from Tommy.

"Thanks, Tom. How are your carrot seeds doing?"

"All watered and ready to grow," he reported with a wide grin. "Tamara made sure I spaced them out just right."

"Excellent!"

"I don't think it's fair that we're all out here digging in the sun, while you're in the shade relaxing with a lemonade," Natasha complained, mud soiling her painted fingernails.

"I offered her dinner, but these were her terms," Nicolas Turner explained, with an amused smile warming his handsome face.

"I solved both your cases," Jordan pointed out. "Though not without a lot of help," Jordan added hastily and in response to a series of glares. "I'll go fetch some more lemonade."

The End

Now that you have finished this cozy mystery, please consider posting a review on Amazon. It would be appreciated.